DEATH OUT OF FOCUS

by William Campbell Gault

With the motion picture industry in crisis, things were so tough for independent director Steve Leander that he was put to it to maintain his mortgage, his swimming pool and his attractive young wife. So, reluctantly, he agreed to direct a picture for Harry Bergdahl, a producer who never lost money on his pix but never got any Oscars either. Then came this insurance investigator Tomkevic with some sinister inquiries about an insurance fix on Bergdahl's lead, Hart Jameson. Soon after, Jameson, a Marlon Brando type, crashed over a cliff on the Coast Highway in his Jaguar, and was killed.

Steve was the man who knew too much. He was hounded by a private eye, mistrusted by his wife, stymied by Bergdahl's slippery financing, and stricken by his own indiscretions. One of the latter, a torrid beauty named Pat Cullum, was fatally stabbed, after some strange revelations about the dead star.

As events developed, Leander was on an even hotter spot with the police breathing down his neck; his position made more risky because of others he felt in conscience he must protect. How he managed to clear himself and finger the real murderer makes a story true to today's Hollywood conditions. It's tough, but the heart is in the right place.

DEATH OUT OF FOCUS

death out of focus

William Campbell Gault

Adams Media
New York London Toronto Sydney New Delhi

Adams Media
An Imprint of Simon & Schuster, Inc.
57 Littlefield Street
Avon, Massachusetts 02322

For information about special discounts for bulk purchases, please contact Simon
& Schuster Special Sales at 1-866-506-1949 or business@simonandschuster.com.

Manufactured in the United States of America

Library of Congress Cataloging-in-Publication Data has been applied for.

ISBN 978-1-4405-5797-2
ISBN 978-1-4405-3918-9 (ebook)

This work has been previously published in print format by:
Random House Publishing, New York, NY.

For Richard Matheson
Whose idea it was

DEATH OUT OF FOCUS

He took the new script out to the sundeck and read it there. He had been in New York for six weeks of frustration; he needed the sun. He tried to blank from his mind all preconceptions, the connotations that a Harry Bergdahl script implied, and read this new one objectively, as a director should.

It was rough going. The script was cliché-ridden, pretentious, pseudo-arty. And yet, when he had finished, some vitality, some sense of truth born of the writer's intensity, stayed with him. A revision by a competent screenwriter could make a worth-while story out of this.

He would probably have to fight Harry on that. It would be logical to guess Bergdahl would want to strengthen the wrong elements and delete the worth-while ones in this tale of a young rebel.

There was a current and comparatively profitable twin tide running in the industry, science fiction stories and stories of adolescent revolt. Harry Bergdahl was a man who had maintained his solvency by never running against the tides. There was a rumor lately that his credit wasn't as sound as it had been, and Steve meant to investigate that rumor. If it weren't true, this call from the producer might well be the luckiest break for Steve in the past year.

It had been a bad year. He was thinking back on it when his housekeeper came out to tell him Mr. Bergdahl was calling. He didn't want to talk with Harry yet. But he took a deep breath and went into the house.

Before Bergdahl could ask, he said quickly, "I haven't had time to do any more than glance through the script, Harry. I've been tied up with New York all morning."

A momentary silence, and "Oh . . . ? You want to ring me when you've read it? I'll be here most of the day."

"I'll do that." A pause. "Who is the writer? He's new to me."

"My nephew," Bergdahl said. "A very talented boy. He's got three credits."

"Story or screenplay?"

"Two story, one screenplay. Why, Steve?"

"I wondered. Just browsing through it, there seems to be a buried strength that doesn't quite come through. A little doctoring would bring it out, I'm sure."

"We can talk about that. And I've got the lead all lined up." A theatrical pause. "Hart Jameson."

Steve had never heard of Hart Jameson. But he said admiringly, "You *have* been busy, haven't you?"

Bergdahl chuckled. "You get to that script right away and then phone me, Steve. We're going to have a picture."

"I'll do that. Good-bye, Harry."

He went back to the sundeck and picked up the script again. He read: "Story by David Louis Sidney." Was it Cabell who had said writers with three names are dead —or ought to be? What kind of a man was David Louis Sidney? Coöperative? He would need to be, or they would have a real lemon of a picture. And Steve couldn't afford any lemons this year.

He decided to have a talk with John Abbot before

4

phoning Bergdahl again. He hadn't visited him for months, and today would be a good time. He was going out to his car, when the green Pontiac pulled into his driveway.

Steve stood in front of the garage door as the man behind the wheel got out and walked toward him. He was tall and slim, with black hair in a crew cut.

His voice was as soft as his brown eyes. "Mr. Leander, Steven Leander?"

"That's right."

"My name is Tomkevic." He handed Steve a card. "Do you have a minute or two right now?"

Steve glanced at the card, saw the words "Veritable Insurance Company" and said, "I'm afraid I don't. My insurance needs are well taken care of, Mr. Tomkevic."

The tall man smiled. "You didn't read *all* of the card, Mr. Leander. I'm not a salesman. I'm an investigator."

"Oh . . . ? Checking one of the neighbors?"

Tomkevic shook his head. "Checking on a Mr. Harry Bergdahl."

Steve frowned, and stared at the man. "I don't understand."

"He's applied for insurance, the regular studio coverage, on a man named Hart Jameson. We handle a lot of this kind of insurance, you understand, Mr. Leander, but not usually to the tune of a quarter of a million on an *unknown* actor."

"Unknown?" Steve smiled. "Are you a movie fan, too, Mr. Tomkevic?"

"I am. I have to be, with the company I work for specializing in this kind of policy. Jameson's had some good reviews on the bits he's done, but he's still an unknown as far as the money people are concerned."

"I see. I thought it was Bergdahl you were investigating, not Jameson."

"It *is* Mr. Bergdahl. I'm going to be frank, Mr. Lean-

5

der. He's never covered any of his other actors. Doesn't that seem strange, when you consider the money he's made on his pictures? And now, with rocky times in the industry, he comes up with this policy."

"I have a feeling," Steve said slowly, "that you're not being quite as frank as you promised. What's on your mind, Mr. Tomkevic?"

"First, he told us he had hired you as director. This morning I learned that wasn't true."

"It's true every way but technically," Steve said. "We had a rather firm oral agreement. Does my connection with the picture change the policy risk in any way?"

Tomkevic nodded. "My employers seem to think so. Your integrity is rather well known in the industry, Mr. Leander." His smile was thin. "You've—never worked with Mr. Bergdahl before, have you?"

"Never. Are you implying that Mr. Bergdahl's reputation isn't all it should be?"

"Do I need to?"

There was a long silence. Finally Steve said, "That was frank enough. But what can I tell you? As you've just said, I've never worked with Harry before. So what can I know about him?"

Tomkevic shrugged. "Not much, I suppose. This much you can tell me—are you going to direct the picture?"

"I think I am. Of course, terms would need to be worked out through my agent that will be acceptable to both of us, but the way it looks now, I'm going to do the picture."

Tomkevic nodded. "Well, I guess we can stall him until everything is signed. That's what I'll suggest to my firm, at any rate." He waved. "Thanks for your time, Mr. Leander." He went back to his car.

So Harry was insuring his young rebel. As a promo-

6

tion gimmick undoubtedly. Harry didn't have enough regard for actors to consider any of them worth more than the trouble of replacing them. But why should that bother an insurance company that specialized in this unique kind of term coverage? Certainly, all of the policies of this kind were at least partially drawn for promotional reasons.

He got into his car and headed it for John Abbot's. Abbot lived in the hills above Hollywood and had lived there for forty years. He was distantly related to Steve's wife, Marcia, and had been influential in Steve's early success.

He had been a writer, director and producer but was now retired. He was, however, often consulted by those still active in the industry. He was in the front yard of his home, supervising the work of a Japanese gardener, when Steve drove up.

He came down to the car and said smilingly, "Trouble, I'll bet. I never see you otherwise. How's my Marcia?"

"She's fine," Steve said. "I'm sorry I haven't been around lately, John. I've been—scrambling."

Abbot nodded. "Everybody in the industry is. Stay for lunch and talk with an old man."

Steve got out of the car and came around it to walk toward the house with his host. "I had some New York work that looked as if it might lead somewhere. But it didn't. It's a rough time, isn't it?"

"Maybe we need some tough times," Abbot said. "Maybe some good pictures will result."

"Maybe," Steve said. "But scared people don't usually make good pictures."

The house was dim and cool, as one came in from the glare of the day outside. From the living-room windows, the entire city was visible in three directions.

7

"Martini?" Abbot asked.

Steve nodded. "John, Harry Bergdahl wants me to direct a picture for him."

From the liquor cabinet Abbot chuckled. "No wonder you're all wound up. I hope you realize he needs you more than you need him."

Steve turned to stare at the older man. "Bergdahl . . . ? He's certainly solid enough. He never lost money on a picture, I've heard."

"Until his last two," Abbot said quietly. "Times have changed, and I don't think Harry has. He's a hangover from the days when the public would look at anything that moved."

"Lousy pictures are still being made, and some of them are making money," Steve argued.

Abbot brought him his drink. "Horror pictures, science fiction pictures, adolescent revolt pictures. How long will the public's stomach stand for those?"

Steve sipped his drink and said wryly, "I hope the public's stomach is stronger than you think, because the picture Harry plans is an adolescent revolt epic."

"But he's smart enough to know it needs the Leander touch. And I'm sure he'll promote the prestige value of that credit reading 'Directed by Steven Leander.'" Abbot sat down with his drink. "Steve, be careful."

"Of Harry?"

"That's right. He is going to survive. If you need him now, in order to continue functioning, work for him. These aren't times when a man can be choosy. *But be very damned careful.*"

"I'm not an innocent, John. I'm sure I can protect myself against any manipulations of Harry Bergdahl."

"Maybe. Where is he getting his money?"

Steve finished his drink. "It's Texas money, oil money." He looked at his empty glass.

8

"Mix your own," Abbot said. "Is the money actually committed?"

"I'm not sure." He went over to mix a drink.

"I asked," Abbot said quietly, "because I heard a silly rumor about Harry insuring Hart Jameson for some picture he'd planned."

Steve turned. "He's trying to insure Jameson. Do you know anything about him?"

Abbot nodded. "He was in *Sunburst Alley*. He has all of Mr. Brando's mannerisms and none of his talent. I can't believe an actor of his caliber is worth too much insuring."

He paused and continued. "You know, Steve, the sole purpose of a studio policy is to insure the picture against anything that might prevent its star from appearing. Injuries, loss of memory, death—whatever might affect shooting or cause expensive delays—are covered. The star happens to be the property involved, and his assessed value determines the need, even the amount of the policy."

"But times being what they are, just suppose—just suppose, you understand—that Bergdahl needing the money—an accident *should* happen to Jameson."

"You don't mean——" said Steve, "that Harry would. . . ?"

"I don't say so. I only raise the question."

"Oh no, you're wrong. It's only a promotional gimmick. It's not the first time that's been pulled, is it?"

"Of course not," Abbot said mildly. "It's just the first time it's been pulled by Harry Bergdahl."

Steve said irritatedly, "For heaven's sake, you make Harry sound like a—monster. He's not our first citizen, I'll grant you, but he's certainly not a—a murderer."

"Not unless he needs to be to survive," Abbot said blandly. "Let's eat and talk about something else."

It was a fine lunch and they didn't talk any more

about Harry Bergdahl. Abbot dwelt, as was his habit lately, on his early days in the industry. Today, Steve listened absently, his mind on the picture.

Finally Abbot said, "All right, you may go now. You've been itching to, for half an hour."

"That's not true," Steve protested. "I enjoy your company and you know it."

"Not when you're ready to start a picture. You have Marcia phone me. Good luck, Steve. Keep in touch, won't you?"

"I certainly will," Steve said warmly and was conscious of half lying. He was at an age where the reminiscences of the old were discomforting. He was thirty-seven.

As he drove home, he reflected that a man of thirty-seven should be solidly established in his trade. At least he should know where his next dollar is coming from. He should be able to turn down offers from hacks like Harry Bergdahl.

He wasn't. So much for that.

He phoned Bergdahl as soon as he arrived home. He told him, "I've read the script now." He took a careful breath. "Your nephew is going to need help on the screenplay."

"We're the boys who can give it to him," Bergdahl answered. "You—weren't suggesting another writer, were you, Steve?"

"Not if this one is coöperative. You know him better than I do, Harry."

"He's young and willing to learn," Bergdahl answered. "He'll make out. I suppose this means you're ready to talk terms?"

"That's my agent's headache," Steve said. "Is the money committed, Harry?"

"Half of it's firm and the other half should be firm in a day or two. Look, why don't you and me and David get together tonight and talk story? Bring Marcia and come over to the house."

"As soon as she gets home, I'll find out if she's free tonight. Shall I phone you then?"

"Not if you're free. If she is, bring her. If she isn't, bring yourself. Dotty would love to see her, though."

Dotty was Harry's latest, and fifth, wife, a bleached sex bomb who had been cultivating Marcia without success for months.

Steve said, "I'll be there. And Marcia probably will, too."

He would have preferred talking with David Louis Sidney alone, but perhaps he could do that later. He picked up the script and went into his study. He was making notes on a few of the script's more painful pretensions when Marcia came home.

She stood in the doorway to the study and said lightly, "I've some gossip for you. I got it from Ellen at lunch."

"I'm all ears."

"It's about Harry Bergdahl. He's found a pair of gullible Texans."

"I know that."

"But you don't know the funny part, I'll bet."

He said patiently, "Tell me the funny part."

"These—cowboys had never heard of any of the pictures Harry had produced. But they knew all the ones you had directed. And Harry told them he had you under contract." She came over to kiss him. "See? Harry needs you more than you need him."

Steve said, "As much, but not more. Marcia, I'm going to do the picture."

"On your terms?"

"On the best terms I can get."

"Why, Steve?"

"Because we have always lived beyond our means

and I need the work. And Harry is the only one who has offered me a job out here in nine months."

She said, "Because you need the work, you are going to go crashing down into oblivion with Harry Bergdahl? That's where he's heading."

"No, he isn't. If anyone survives, Harry will. Now, kiss me again and go mix us a drink."

"In a second," she said. "Is it my fault we're in bad financial shape, Steve?"

"No, it's our fault." He stroked her hair. "I love you, Marcia Bishop Leander."

"I know it," she said. "Why don't we take a swim and then—well, kind of—loll around?"

He smiled at her as desire stirred in him. "I've lolled around with you before. But not in the afternoon, not lately. You're being compassionate."

"Let's go," she said. "Let's forget the future for a few hours."

TWO

It was later, it was six o'clock when he told her, "Dotty Bergdahl is expecting you tonight. I'm going over there for a story conference with Harry and his nephew."

Marcia sighed and stretched on the big bed. "You do demand a lot of me, don't you? An evening with Dotty Bergdahl—ouch!"

"I didn't promise you'd come. I told Harry I wasn't sure if you were free tonight."

"I'll go, master," she whispered. "You have rendered me temporarily docile with your ministrations."

Later, as they drove over to Brentwood, Steve tried to frame words in his mind, words that would be tactful but not servile, words that would help to establish a working agreement for the salvation of that impossible script.

The knowledge that Bergdahl needed him would strengthen his hand. The tradition that the director is king but the producer is God would help to strengthen Bergdahl's.

They were traveling along San Vicente when Marcia said quietly, "Go in there believing you don't *have* to direct this picture. Go in there feeling *big*, because you are."

"Were," he said.

13

"Are. And Harry knows it. Why else would he want you? Out of compassion? Think, Steve."

The house was rustic, board and batten, painted a dusty almond, a U-shaped structure with a circular drive serving the front door and a parking area leading off on the right-hand side.

Dotty and Harry were sitting in the screened front patio having a drink as the Leanders came up the flagstone walk. Harry was in shorts and his thick legs were almost black from the sun.

Dotty was in pale yellow chiffon, looking appealingly summery, but neither chiffon nor a pinafore could disguise her essential and basic attraction.

Sex surged from her appraising eyes, her sinuous movements, her sultry voice. She was no brain, but before settling down with Harry she had attracted some of the gentlemen who passed for brains in this superficial town. She had been squired, also, by old, young and medium-aged male stars whose choice was wide and opportunities endless.

She had a reputation as a girl who truly enjoyed the bed, a rarity among those who used their bodies to aspire to high places. What she lacked in intellect, she more than made up in cunning.

Harry said, "Stop staring at my wife, Steve, and name your poison." He patted a portable bar, complete with mechanical refrigeration. "Dotty's anniversary present to me."

"I had no idea it's been a year," Marcia said.

"It hasn't," Harry said. "Six months, it's been." He winked at Steve. "That's kind of a record for me."

Genial opening touch, Steve thought. *At least we're starting as friends.* He asked casually, "Where's our writer?"

"He'll be along," Harry answered. "I wanted to talk

14

to you first, Steve. You see, Dave's young and kind of artistic and we're going to have to go easy on him."

"A Princeton boy," Dotty put in. "You know how it is with Princeton boys . . ."

Marcia said sweetly, "No. Tell us how it is, Dotty, with Princeton boys?"

For a moment Steve stood rigidly, shocked and frightened.

Then Harry's guffaw broke the tension. "That Marcia! She kills me. Oh man, Steve, you've got one there!"

Steve looked at his wife appraisingly. He had one there, remarks for all occasions, personalities for all gatherings, an astute and daring darling.

"She kills me, too, at times," he admitted and began to breathe again.

They talked about David Louis Sidney then and it was standard enough. David was still conscious of Princeton. He had published a few short stories and one slim novel before coming to work in Hollywood.

Harry said, "He admires you, Steve. I think it would be better, maybe, if you brought him around to our way of thinking. I'm just his dumb uncle, to him."

Steve nodded. He paused before saying, "Harry, how much leeway do I get with this picture?"

Bergdahl looked at his wife and back at Steve. He licked his lips. "I phoned you, didn't I? I know how independent you can be, but I called you. What can I promise? I never had a lemon, Steve; you got to remember that."

"I remember it. And I'm aware that there are a lot of directors currently unemployed. But if we're at cross-purposes, Harry, nothing good can come out of this for either of us."

Bergdahl's smile was purely facial. "You figure me for a dumb uncle, too, huh?"

Steve shook his head. "I find it hard to say what has to be said, Harry. I—want us to understand each other."

Dotty smiled vapidly. Marcia watched them intently. Bergdahl inclined his head back and his big jaw came up almost defiantly. "I can say it. You're artist. I'm the cornball. That's where I built my reputation, on corn. Maybe today the market ain't so good for corn. Maybe I even need you more than you need me. But I raised the money and I'm still the producer. I'll give a lot of thought to every change you want and respect it. But I will still be the producer."

There was a static moment all around before Steve smiled and said, "Harry, I would be extremely uncomfortable any time I sensed that you weren't being *all* producer. I think we're going to get along."

"Sure we are," Bergdahl said jovially. "Hell, yes. Here, let me mix you a drink."

After that, the problem of David Louis Sidney turned out to be no problem at all. He was young and impressionable, and he was a Steven Leander fan. Every suggestion Steve made for a script change was eagerly agreed to by Sidney.

And then, to cap the evening, he told Steve, as he and Marcia were leaving, "I want to say that I consider it a great privilege to be able to work with you, Mr. Leander."

Steve smiled and winked at Harry. He said, "Dave, your uncle will agree with me, I'm sure, when I tell you it is a great privilege to be able to work at all in the industry today."

Harry laughed and Dotty giggled and the Leanders left them laughing.

In the car Marcia said, "You do have the cleverest exit lines. You soaped everyone with that last line, didn't you?"

16

"It was a bone for Harry. It was a winner's gesture, dear."

"I see. Did Harry tell you he had insured this Hart Jameson's life for a quarter of a million dollars?"

"Harry didn't tell me, but I knew he was trying to. The investigator for the insurance company came to see me this morning."

"Why? Why should he come to see you?"

"Because," Steve answered smugly, "he wanted to be sure I'd be connected with the picture. That way, he'd know there'd be no financial shenanigans. On account of my integrity, as he explained."

"Brother . . . !" Marcia said. "Aren't we something!" She took a deep breath. "Steve, you did come out on top, didn't you?"

"Temporarily."

"Is there any hope of making it a—worth-while picture?"

"More now than there was three hours ago. But, as I said, my dominance is only temporary." He paused. "Young Sidney told me that his friends at Princeton considered me one of the three great directors out here."

Marcia yawned. "Maybe he didn't have many friends at Princeton. Don't get smug. Young David may be a fan of yours—but he's Harry's *nephew*."

"I'll never be able to get smug," he assured her. "Not while I'm married to you."

They rode the rest of the way in silence. At home, as the garage door opened and he drove into the lighted garage, Marcia said softly, "We could have saved money, couldn't we? We could be fat and solvent right now if we were different people."

"We're what we are," he said. "You were born rich and I was born hungry."

They walked quietly through the kitchen, through

17

the entry hall and down the hall that led past the children's empty bedrooms. The children were at summer camp.

At their bedroom door, Steve said, "I'm going to sit up for a while. I want to go over that story again."

"Kiss me good night then."

He kissed her.

She said, "It's been a good day, hasn't it, all in all?"

"Pretty good."

"Then why am I frightened?"

"I don't know. Everybody is. *Everybody.* Go to sleep now. Forget about tomorrow."

In his study, he sat for a while without looking at the script, vaguely disturbed. It couldn't be only his temporary insolvency that nagged at him; despite his income through the good years they had always ridden the precarious edge of insolvency. It was a part of the local pattern.

Was there some threat beyond the financial, something in his now almost firm alliance with Harry Bergdahl? Harry was only a man trying to survive and he needed Steven Leander for that. Steve picked up the script and began to read.

He didn't get to bed until two o'clock. And there he had a long and involved dream of searching a mammoth parking lot for his Bentley and not being able to remember where he had parked it. Finally, in his dream, he found the battered, rusty Model T Ford that had been his father's pride for years.

THREE

Hart Jameson's signing for the new picture was mentioned in Hedda Hopper's column next morning. Hedda didn't bite on the promotional gimmick of the insurance policy, but the paper's local cinema columnist gave it a paragraph. In this account Jameson was identified as "that exciting newcomer who caused such a sensation in *Sunburst Alley.*"

Across the breakfast table from him, Marcia said, "You're happy again. You're never happy when you're not functioning, are you?"

"I'm happy," he agreed. "I'm going to take my coffee into the study. Send Dave in when he comes."

Dave Sidney arrived at ten o'clock and they spent the next two hours on the story changes and projected screenplay. Steve had no reason to complain about the young man's willingness to rewrite. What disturbed him was his doubt about Dave's ability to produce credible dialogue. With luck, that could be corrected off the cuff and on the set. With luck—and coöperation from Harry Bergdahl. Some producers could be hard-nosed about sticking to the final shooting script.

He said to Dave, "Lines that look good in print often don't come over when voiced. I hope Harry won't be difficult about any impromptu changes."

David Louis Sidney smiled knowingly. "My uncle

19

isn't going to interfere with you, Steve. Don't give it another thought."

"What made you say that? How can you be sure?"

"I explained it all to Uncle Harry. About your four years of screenwriting and my hope I could learn the trade under you. I have his promise that he won't interfere with us."

"Well," Steve said. "Well, thank you! You've earned yourself a free lunch. We've done enough for one morning."

Everything was working out. There would be some friction, he knew, but the basic conflicts he had anticipated were not developing. The enthusiasm he needed came back.

He viewed some film on Hart Jameson that afternoon. The youth was photogenic and intense. His technique showed a gaucherie that careful direction could eliminate.

Steve came home to his dinner well pleased with his day. His agent had battled to an advantageous contract with Harry, and he knew his star was going to work out.

He came home to his dinner and a phone call from Laura Spain. She had been the star of his first picture, and the box-office magic of her name had been an important part of the picture's success. She had required masterful make-up to play an ingénue even then; she cherished the illusion that she still could.

She said brightly, "I'm looking for work, Steve, and I heard you were casting a Harry Bergdahl picture."

"All the good parts are cast, Laura," he lied.

A silence and then she said quietly, "I'm not looking for a *good* part. I'm looking for *work*, Steve. I mean any kind of work."

Embarrassment touched him. "Don't talk like that. Your name has value only as long as you think it has."

"I'm not thinking of my name these days," she said. "I'm really broke."

His embarrassment deepened but he kept his voice casual. "In that case, let's talk about it. Why don't you come over and have dinner with us? We'd love to see you again. We'll be eating in about an hour."

"I'll be there," she promised, "with last year's bells on. I'm serious about needing work, Steve."

"We'll talk about it," he said.

Marcia was out at the pool. Steve went out to tell her Laura was coming for dinner.

"She phoned twice this afternoon," Marcia told him. "I hope you're not soft enough to give her a job in that picture."

He stared at his wife. "Why the sudden animosity? I thought you liked Laura."

"I do. But she is perhaps the world's third worst actress, as both of us know."

"She's a star," Steve explained, "not an actress. Often, that's more important. Anyone can learn to act. Stars are born."

"Loyal, loyal Steve," Marcia teased. "Mix me a martini."

Laura came before they had finished their drinks. She was still fashionably slim and her face still held the delicate bone structure that had been her fortune.

She kissed Marcia and held Steve's hand for a long time. Steve asked, "Drink?"

She shook her head sadly. "No, thank you. Not an ounce for eleven months. It was—becoming—a problem." Her smile was falsely bright. "That's just between us, of course."

Steve felt the same empathic embarrassment he had felt while talking with her on the phone. Now, in sudden decision, he said, "I've been thinking of you since we talked, Laura. I wouldn't be surprised if you could handle the mother in this epic. Are you ready for mothers?"

"I'm ready for maids," she said. "I'm strapped, honey."

"Well, don't admit it to Harry Bergdahl," he advised her. "I'm going to phone him right now."

Harry wasn't home. Dotty told Steve that he was out on the town with his Texans, and heaven only knew when he would be home.

"Would you have him call me, honey, if he gets in before midnight? I've just had an inspirational idea for casting the mother in our masterpiece."

"I'll tell him, sweet," Dotty answered. A pause. "Give my love to Marcia—if she's listening."

Steve hung up and smiled at his wife. "Dotty sends her love. *If* you're listening."

Marcia sniffed. "And what was the 'honey' for? That's not Leander terminology."

"Dotty isn't standard," Steve explained. He looked at Laura. "Right, Miss Spain?"

"I'll say she isn't," Laura agreed. "That's how Harry is able to sign up these young actors so cheaply. They all come over to sniff around Dotty. That's how he hooked Hart Jameson. And Brad Amherst—for that last horror picture of his."

Steve finished his drink and said, "You're an incurable gossip, Laura. Let's get to the food."

It was an enjoyable dinner, spiced by the reminiscences of Laura's classic and multitudinous feuds, warmed by nostalgia for a better time.

At eleven-thirty Bergdahl returned his call. Steve said, "I think I can get Laura Spain for the mother. How does that sound to you, Harry?"

22

"Expensive," Bergdahl answered. "Look, I'm a little drunko right now. Let's talk about it tomorrow."

Steve hung up and faced the anxious gaze of Laura. He said, "Harry's too drunk to think tonight. He did say he thought you might be expensive."

"But he's interested?"

"I'm sure he is. Now don't fret about it. You get a good night's sleep, and Harry will probably phone your agent in the morning."

She leaned over to kiss him. "Bless you, Steve. You're one of the anointed."

In the dark and quiet house Steve lay awake, planning. He thought of the children, away at summer camp; he thought of his Sue, aged nine, away from home for the first year, sleeping so far from him.

He thought of Harry Bergdahl and John Abbot and Laura and Dotty. He fell asleep thinking about Dotty and was glad that Marcia couldn't read his mind.

In the morning he had another session with Dave Sidney that went well. Dave's ineptness was due to lack of experience, not lack of discernment, and Steve no longer worried about their ability to work together.

He phoned Harry right after lunch and Harry told him, "I was talking to Dotty about Laura Spain. Dotty thinks she's poison for a picture."

Steve kept his voice casual. "I see. And what do *you* think about her, Harry?"

A pause. "I don't know. Have her come in and talk to me, huh? Maybe, if she's cheap enough . . ."

"I'll call her agent," Steve said. "Everything else going all right, Harry?"

Another pause. "You heard something different?"

"Not a thing," Steve said lightly. "Should I have heard something different?"

23

"I'm having a little trouble with one of my pigeons. I worked on him four hours last night. Could you raise some quick money, Steve?"

Was this a test, a gauge of Steve's need? He said easily, "I couldn't even raise any slow money, Harry. Uncle Sam is living in my pocket."

"Ain't it the truth?" Harry said. "Well, don't worry. Half of it is solid, and the other boy is beginning to soften. You get together with Dave and get that script straightened around. Okay?"

"Right," Steve said.

Then he went into Hollywood to have lunch with his agent, and learned he was lucky to be working. All the live drama shows on TV were being dropped; the filmed shows already under the control of various studio hacks. Hollywood exhibitor production was down forty percent from the corresponding period of last year, and last year hadn't been a world-beater.

This picture had to be made and it had to be successful. Viewing it as objectively as possible, Steve knew it could easily be the most important crisis in his career.

FOUR

They began shooting on a Monday, and the first straw in the wind was the nonappearance of Hart Jameson. Steve had talked with Jameson Friday and learned he had signed his contract. The lad had made no mention of not being able to make the Monday call.

At ten o'clock Bergdahl told Steve to go ahead with the scenes that didn't include Jameson. Steve had spent the day working with Laura and the other principals.

He was working with a cast of highly receptive professionals and a cameraman who knew his trade. Things went as well as anyone could expect for a first day's shooting.

Tuesday and Wednesday they were on location in Santa Barbara, and five more days of shooting had been planned for that city. Hart Jameson had not appeared.

Wednesday evening Laura came back from Santa Barbara in Steve's car. It had been a grueling day, hot and full of retakes, and Laura was unusually quiet.

As they came into Ventura, Steve said, "You're doing very well, trouper. Was I rough on you today?"

"No. Even when you are, you always make sense to me. I was thinking about Jameson, wondering about him. Aren't you?"

"Yes. But no gossip now. It's been a hot day."

"All right," she said wearily. "*All right!*"

25

They were past Ventura and approaching Oxnard when Steve said, "Okay, let's have it."

Laura took a breath. "Well, first, you know he had a criminal record, of course?"

"Not quite a *criminal* record. A juvenile delinquency record a few years back, yes."

"So a record, anyway. Tie that up with this insurance policy Harry took out on him. And some drunken bragging Jameson did at a party a few nights ago to a friend of mine. Hart said he might just possibly have a little accident in his Jaguar, something that might injure his back."

"Kid talk," Steve scoffed. "I hope he doesn't think a faked back injury would fool those insurance doctors."

"Maybe he does. And maybe Harry does, too." Laura paused. "You knew that one of Harry's angels backed out, didn't you?"

"No." Steve slowed the car. "Laura, you're not *looking* for trouble, are you?"

She shook her head slowly. "I've had enough trouble to last me the rest of my life. All I want is to keep working."

"We both have to keep working," Steve said quietly. "I think we had better forget we ever had this conversation."

"I've already forgotten it," she said. "And my friend told nobody but me. She *claims*. Don't you think you should have a talk with Harry Bergdahl, though?"

"I intend to, tonight," Steve said. "We can't continue to shoot around Jameson indefinitely."

The financial shenanigans of Harry Bergdahl were not his business, Steve tried to tell himself. His job was to direct a picture and make it the best picture that could be made with the people and money committed to it. Finance was the producer's realm and the producer's problem.

26

He dropped Laura off in Brentwood and reminded her, "Forget about Jameson's drunken bragging. Let's concentrate on the problems we have on the set."

She nodded. She patted his hand before stepping from the car.

It was the housekeeper's half-day, and Marcia was in the kitchen preparing dinner when Steve came home.

"Your drink's in the refrigerator," she said. "How did it go today?"

"Fine. That Laura's a real pro. I'm glad I cast her."

"There's something else on your mind. I can tell."

"Nothing," he said irritably. He went to the refrigerator. "It's been hot up there in Santa Barbara."

"It's been hot here, too. I see in the *Times* that your star got into a bar brawl last night."

He turned from the refrigerator. "Jameson?"

She nodded. "The paper's in the living room. It's on the front page. The picture was mentioned."

He didn't go to the living room. He sat at the kitchen table and sipped his drink.

Marcia asked casually, "How is David Louis Sidney doing?"

"Well. I enjoy working with Dave. We understand each other."

"And he's good for your ego," Marcia added. "You haven't kissed me yet, big man."

"I'm too tired to get up," he told her. "Come over here and I'll kiss you."

She came over to kiss him. She stroked his hair and said, "There's a letter from the kids. I think they miss us. Could we go up there Sunday?"

He nodded.

She massaged the back of his neck. "Do you want to tell me what's bothering you, now?"

"Nothing serious. I'm in a complicated business and

27

it has a million tedious problems and a million minor decisions every day. I'm bushed, that's all."

"Has Harry been giving you trouble?"

"He hasn't opened his mouth. He's giving me less trouble than I imagined in my rosiest dreams."

She leaned over to kiss him again. "All right, working man, I'll get off your back. Let's eat outside like the Corn Belt refugees."

He stayed in the shower a long time, letting the warm spray relax his neck and shoulder muscles, trying to dissolve his problems and his doubts in the soapy water that gurgled through the drain at his feet.

He had always tried to divorce himself from the gossip, the rumors, the angle shooting that was the sustenance of so many in the industry. Perhaps it was not wise to stay too aloof from the machinations of his contemporaries.

Marcia was setting the table on the sundeck when he came out from the dressing room. He went into the study and dialed Hart Jameson's number.

Jameson's voice was faintly blurred and annoyingly jovial. "I'll bet you're worried about me. Don't be. The bum didn't lay a hand on me."

"I'm worried about the picture," Steve said.

Over the wire came a muffled, feminine giggle and a less muffled, feminine "Stop that!"

Steve said stiffly, "I hope I'm not interrupting anything. Would it be possible for me to see you tonight?"

Jameson chuckled. "It all depends. This one may take some time to get to. She's the coy type. Does Harry want to talk to me, too?"

"I don't know," Steve answered. "I—heard a rumor and I want your version of it. But not over a phone."

Silence for a few moments, and then Jameson said, "Why not drop over here? It's not far. I can always send

28

the—company out for another bottle or some ciga-rettes."

Steve carefully kept the indignation from his voice. "Would eight-thirty be all right?"

"Dandy," Jameson said. "Don't forget to knock."

Steve sat by the phone a few minutes before going out to the deck. He told Marcia, "I'm going over to see Jameson tonight. I'll only be gone for about an hour."

"*That's* what's been bothering you," she declared. "I knew there was something."

He didn't argue with her. He sat quietly in the shade of the overhang, looking down at his neighbors. Beyond the house immediately below, the canyon wound, dry and gray, lined with stunted chaparral. In the flood season the canyon would run high with water, and the hills would be green.

Marcia must have been reading his thoughts. She said, "All this country really needs is summer rain."

"Summer rain," he agreed, "and a tenth as many people and some New England thrift."

She made a face. "I could start using oleomargarine."

"Bring me another drink," he said. "I'm beginning to feel almost human."

The apartment of Hart Jameson was on the second floor of a stucco building in a less desirable section of Brentwood. Mr. Jameson's success was recent, and his address obviously had not caught up with it.

Steve heard voices before he turned the mechanical chime in the door. Silence followed the chime and then Jameson called, "Just a minute."

It seemed longer than that before the door opened and the bright brown eyes of Hart Jameson considered Steve genially. "Eight-thirty on the dot. I'm not used to punctual people." He stood aside. "Come in."

Steve came into a small living room smelling of gin, perfume and cigarette smoke. A short hall to the right served the bedroom and bath. The bedroom door was closed.

Steve said meaningly, "I'd hoped to catch you alone."

"You did," Jameson said. "I'm all by my lonesome."

Steve hesitated and then headed for a studio couch at the far end of the room from the small hall. He sat down and looked around the room and up at Jameson.

"Speak freely," the youth assured him. "We're alone."

Steve kept his voice low. "I heard a very silly rumor at a party the other night. I heard you were planning a back injury."

Jameson's blunt-featured face twisted in a grin. "You hear the damnedest things at parties, don't you? I was figuring it even heavier than that. I figured to roll the Jag once over lightly to give it some realism. No risk. I used to roll my souped flivver all the time."

"Don't," Steve warned quietly. "You'd never get away with it. Those insurance investigators are extremely able men, Hart."

Jameson chuckled. "So we had another idea. I could run her off a cliff and then go down on foot, tear up my clothes a little and scuff around in the dirt. I don't worry about the Jag. She's insured to the hilt."

Steve almost whispered, "You said 'we.' Who else is involved in this absurd idea?"

Jameson smiled. "Now, who would be? Who's kept me out of the shooting all along?"

"Harry. Is this *his* idea?"

"I'm not going to say it," Jameson answered. "Look, what's all this to you? You're the great artist. The money isn't your department."

"It's not as simple as a question of raising money," Steve answered. "It's a question of morality."

Jameson shrugged. "Oh, come on . . . ! *Morality,*

where a billion-dollar insurance company is involved?
That's cutting it real thin, man."

"Their morality isn't involved," Steve explained.
"Yours is. And something that might be more important to you—your future. What you plan is already a
rumor. If you go through with it, the rumor will be sub-
stantiated. Your career could be finished."

Jameson shook his head. "You know, I got a couple of
real cornball opinions left over from my kid days. And
one of them is that talent will *always* make out. I may
not be any Brando, but I sure as hell got more on the
ball than most of the slobs that are coining it today."

Steve nodded. "I'll buy that. And this picture could do
a lot for your career."

Jameson laughed. "Come *on!* Man, I read that miserable script. This is going to be a dog to end all dogs.
Level with me. It stinks, right?"

"No," Steve said firmly. "Originally, it was an un-
realized story. It's been fixed now, and the rushes have
been impressive."

Silence. Jameson stared at him in doubt. To Steve's
nostrils came the odor of that unusual perfume again,
stronger than the gin or cigarette smoke.

Jameson said, "You're leveling? I got a lot of regard
for your opinion, man. I saw every picture you ever
directed. That's why I couldn't figure you on this dog."

"It's not going to be a great picture," Steve said
quietly, "but it's going to be a good one. And more important to you at this stage in your career, it's going to
be financially successful."

Jameson sat down at the other end of the studio couch
and lighted a cigarette. Belatedly he offered one to
Steve.

Steve shook his head.

Jameson said softly, "I could have been conned, you
know? It happens all the time in this town, right?"

31

Steve nodded.

After a moment Jameson said, "I promise nothing. And for the record, I admit nothing, either. But I'm going to do some thinking. I'll call you tomorrow night, right?"

Steve stood up. "Do that." He smiled. "And Mr. Self-Admitted Talent, I'll tell you something else. You have enough on the ball, but also a big fat need for good direction."

Jameson grinned. "From maybe three people in this phony town, I'd take that remark. You're one of 'em. Go home and rest easy now. And this little visit stays a secret between us, huh?"

Steve nodded and then looked again at the closed bedroom door.

"Rest easy," Jameson repeated. "Leave the finagling to the guys that live by it."

It wasn't bad advice, Steve reflected, but it had come a little late. If Jameson had a change of heart now and appeared for the picture, perhaps there would be no picture. The involved financial shenanigans of Harry Bergdahl were too complicated for an amateur to tamper with.

But he felt better for having made the trip. Laura's rumor had proved to be factual, and it was possible he had saved a talented young man from committing a disastrous act. He smiled at his own pomposity. What he had probably done was to jam the financial machinery that would have kept him solvent.

At home Marcia said, "You look smug. What happened?"

"I did my good deed for the day. Why don't we go to a movie? Movies are better than ever, I heard."

"I thought you were bushed."

"Not any more. Let's go. I'm restless."

It was a long show and well after midnight before

32

they left the theatre. Then Marcia developed a gnawing urge for a hamburger, so they stopped at a drive-in.

Consequently, it was after one o'clock when they drove up the long and winding road that led to their hilltop home.

The lights of the Bentley illuminated a little MG as they swung around the last curve, and Marcia said, "Isn't that Dave Sidney's car? What would he be doing here this time of the night?"

"This town is full of MG's," Steve answered. "It must be someone visiting a neighbor."

"It's Dave," Marcia insisted. "See? He's getting out of the car."

She was right. Dave Sidney stood next to his car now, watching their headlights. Then, as Steve swung into the driveway, Dave came across the lawn toward them.

Steve killed the engine and got out. "What's the matter, Dave? Trouble?"

"Plenty," Dave answered. "Uncle Harry sent me over. He's been phoning you for an hour. Hart Jameson's had an accident."

Steve stood rigidly, staring through the darkness at Dave's face, barely visible in the reflection from the headlights. "My God! I talked with him earlier this evening." He paused. "Was he injured seriously?"

"His car went over the bluff above the Coast Highway in the Palisades," Dave said softly. "He was killed."

FIVE

For seconds Steve stood there quietly, unable to speak. Then he said, "Let's go into the house. Let's not stand out here."

Marcia put the car away as Steve and Dave walked toward the front door.

Dave asked, "Was Hart sober when you talked with him?"

"He'd been drinking, I'm sure," Steve said hesitantly. "Dave, I'm trying to decide whether or not I should tell you *why* I went to see Jameson tonight."

Dave stopped walking. "You went to see him? For some reason, I got the impression you talked with him over the phone."

Steve shook his head. "I went to his apartment. And I'm going to tell you why. Right here, without Marcia. I don't want her to know about it."

He told Dave about the rumor but not where he had heard it. He told him about the talk with Jameson and about hearing the voices before he went into the apartment and about the perfume.

When he'd finished, he said, "Except for the girl, I could be the last man to see him alive. I suppose I had better tell the police about it."

"And the rumor, too?" Dave asked.

"I don't know. I can't decide about that. It could make your uncle look bad, couldn't it?"

"It could easily cost him a quarter of a million dollars," Dave said. "Uncle Harry is no angel, Steve, but I can't see him as a murderer. Can you?"

Steve said no and knew he was lying.

"What must have happened," Dave went on, "is that Jameson got stinking drunk and had an actual accident. I don't see what else it could be. He certainly didn't commit suicide in order to accommodate Uncle Harry. But if this rumor gets out, the insurance company has a case."

"That's true," Steve agreed. "I don't know what good . . ."

From the doorway Marcia asked, "Can't you two talk in the house? Is there something I shouldn't know?"

"A number of things," Dave said lightly. "This is all dull man talk."

She looked between them anxiously. "Something's wrong. Is it about the insurance?"

Steve said calmly, "No, honey. We'll be in in a minute. Why don't you put some coffee on?"

Again she looked between them. Then, without speaking, she closed the door.

Steve said, "I should tell the police I talked with Jameson tonight, don't you think? That girl could tell them I was there, and they might wonder why I didn't phone them."

"If they ask you," Dave said, "you can tell them. And I'm sure they'll ask you. I'm too young to be giving you advice, Steve, but if I were in your position, I'd sit tight until somebody else opened."

They stood in silence for a moment. The headlights of a car grew brighter as it came up the hill.

Dave said softly, "I could never understand the mechanics or morality of money, and I'm sure it's a con-

35

fusion we share, Steve. This much you know, *you* haven't done anything wrong."

The car turned off at a driveway and they were in darkness again. Steve said, "Let's go in and have some coffee."

Dave nodded. "And I'd better phone Uncle Harry."

Marcia had the electric percolator bubbling on the counter in the breakfast room. From the other room they could hear Dave dialing his uncle's number. Steve stared at the bright chrome of the percolator.

Marcia said quietly, "It can't possibly be anything I shouldn't know about."

He transferred his stare to her. "What can't?"

"Whatever you're being so secretive about. Whatever you and Dave were whispering about outside."

From the other room Dave called, "Uncle Harry wants to talk with you, Steve."

Bergdahl's voice was worried. "Dave tells me you talked to Jameson tonight."

"That's right, Harry."

"What about? Was he despondent or anything? I mean—do you think it could have been suicide?"

"I doubt it. I went over to his apartment to check a rumor I'd heard."

"Oh . . . ? What kind of rumor?"

"One I'd rather not voice"—he paused—"over a phone."

There was a silence which seemed to stretch. Then Bergdahl said quietly, "It looks bad—him not being in any of the shooting yet. It will look bad to the insurance people."

"It looks bad," Steve agreed. He took a breath. "Though we really didn't need him this early."

Harry sounded relieved. "That's right. You'll vouch for that. Well, I can handle 'em. I wonder what happened . . . ?"

36

"I'm wondering, too, Harry. We'll talk about it to-morrow. I think we both need a good night's sleep."

"You'd better stay up for a while," Bergdahl told him. "A Sergeant Morrow is on his way over to see you right now."

Apprehension moved through Steve. "A policeman?"

"That's right. A detective from Homicide, yet. Don't ask me why."

Steve hung up and sat quietly by the phone, and realized with some shame that he wasn't thinking about the dead Hart Jameson at the moment. He was thinking of the picture.

The picture must be saved. Hart Jameson was dead; nothing could help him now.

In the breakfast room Dave was telling Marcia, ". . . And one Texan stayed in but the other backed out. Uncle Harry has more than half the money he needs, though."

Marcia asked coolly, "Would the insurance on Hart Jameson make up the rest?"

Steve glared at his wife. Dave Sidney looked uncomfortable.

Marcia said, "I'm sorry, Dave." She met Steve's glare defiantly.

Steve said, "There's a detective coming over to see me. A Sergeant Morrow—from Homicide."

Nobody said anything for seconds. Then Dave said lamely, "I'd better go. I'll see you tomorrow, I suppose, Steve."

Marcia went to the door with him as Steve sat down and poured himself a cup of coffee. How much of his dialogue with Hart Jameson should he repeat to Sergeant Morrow? How much of it had that girl in the other room overheard?

Jameson had as much as admitted that the rumor was true. But when he had left Jameson this evening,

Steve had felt sure he had convinced the youth the whole scheme was absurd and dangerous.

Tonight's accident might have been a catastrophic coincidence. But if he told Sergeant Morrow about their dialogue . . . ?

He heard the front door close and then Marcia came back to the breakfast room. "I think I'll go to bed. I think you've made it plain that you won't need me tonight."

He looked at her dully. "You're being ridiculous."

"Perhaps. I'm tired. I'm going to bed."

He didn't look at her. He sipped his coffee. For a moment, she stood in the doorway, staring at him. He wanted to look up, to ask her to stay. But he didn't.

She turned and left him.

In his mind Steve damned Harry Bergdahl and his financial shenanigans. In his mind, he framed words for Sergeant Morrow. And he realized he had already made his moral decision when he had told Bergdahl that they hadn't needed Jameson in the early shooting.

Mortgages and Magnin's and the new Bentley . . . The picture must be saved.

Sergeant Morrow was a bony man with gray hair and a weary horse's face. A shorter, stockier man was with him, a Detective Sommers.

Steve said, "I was just having some coffee. I can imagine both of you gentlemen could use a cup about now."

Morrow looked at Sommers and Sommers nodded. They all went into the breakfast room. The officers sat where they would be facing Steve.

As he poured Morrow's coffee, Steve said, "I talked with Hart Jameson earlier this evening. He had been drinking then."

"On the phone?" Morrow asked.

Steve shook his head. "I went to see him. I—read about that bar brawl he'd been in and I thought a little advice wouldn't be amiss."

Morrow asked, "Was he alone?"

Steve frowned. "I couldn't swear in court that he wasn't. But I heard him talking to a woman before I rang his bell and I'm sure she was in another room all the time I was there."

"What time was this?"

"I got there at eight-thirty. I stayed about fifteen minutes."

Morrow sipped his coffee. Sommers sipped his coffee. Steve said, "I get the impression Jameson's death isn't considered accidental. Is there a suspicion of murder?"

Morrow said dryly, "When a quarter of a million dollars is involved, there's always a suspicion of murder." He looked at Steve bleakly. "Wouldn't that make sense to you?"

Steve didn't answer. His mouth was dry. Even then he thought only of the picture.

Sommers said, "You can be damned sure there'll be an insurance dick camped in your hair for a while. If you've got anything that might help us, now would be a real bright time to speak up."

"There's nothing I can think of," Steve said quietly. "Absolutely nothing."

They talked for only a few minutes after that. Both detectives finished their coffee and stood up. Morrow said, "We've got a full night ahead of us. We'll be back tomorrow, Mr. Leander."

"I'll be on location in Santa Barbara all day," Steve said.

"Why?" Morrow asked. "You won't be going ahead with the picture until you get a new star, will you?"

"We'll be going ahead with the picture," Steve answered. "We can always get another actor."

Morrow paused for a moment before saying, "We'll keep in touch with you. Good night."

Steve went to the door with them. After he closed it, he waited until he had heard their car pulling away. Then he went into the bedroom. Marcia was asleep or feigning sleep. He didn't disturb her.

His lies didn't seem to affect his own sleep; he dropped off as soon as his head hit the pillow.

He was at the breakfast table when Bergdahl phoned in the morning. Harry said, "I've had agents on my neck since the morning paper came out. Goddamned vultures . . . ! What do you think of Tom Leslie for Jameson's part?"

"I think we'd be lucky to get him. Do I go to Santa Barbara today?"

"Why not?"

Steve said nothing.

Harry asked, "How long did the law stay last night?"

"Only long enough for a cup of coffee. I have a feeling that the insurance investigators are going to give it more time than that."

"Why . . . ? Jesus, the punk had a record of drunken driving. And a criminal record, too."

Again Steve said nothing.

Bergdahl asked sharply, "Is there something on your mind, Steve? What's on your mind?"

"Hart Jameson, of course. He had a tendency to brag, Harry."

"I heard about that. So all punks brag. Cripes, man, you don't think I killed the kid, do you?"

"I'm wondering what the police will think."

"Think, think, think . . . ! Who cares what anybody thinks? *Proof*—that's what the judge listens to."

40

Harry lowered his voice. "Listen, you worry about the picture. That's enough to worry about. I'll worry about the money. Okay, Steve?"

"Fair enough," Steve said. "Are we agreed on Tom Leslie for the part?"

"I'll let you know. I won't sign anybody until I let you know. Now, remember, all you think about is the picture. You forget about everything else, okay?"

"Okay, Harry. Good luck."

"Yeh. Oh, yeh. Good-bye."

Steve came back to the breakfast table and the *Times* account of the Jameson tragedy, complete with pictures. There was a view of the cliff over which the Jaguar had tumbled and a picture of the battered car lying on its side on the Coast Highway.

It was early and Marcia was still in bed. He ate alone. He read that an autopsy was planned and that the police were searching for two people: the girl who was reported to have been with Jameson before the accident and an unidentified man who had been seen in the exclusive area on top of the bluff from which the car had fallen.

There was no reason given why an unidentified man should not be in the area. Steve assumed the police had more reason than his presence to be suspicious of him. The police weren't likely to reveal all of their information to the newspapers.

None of it was his business, he told himself firmly. He had a picture to make. He had Hart Jameson's part to cast and Laura Spain's jitters to look forward to. Laura had voiced that rumor only fourteen hours ago. And now Hart Jameson was dead. If they could get Tom Leslie for the part . . .

Before leaving to pick up Laura, he went into the bedroom to see if Marcia was awake. She wasn't. She was lying on her back, her eyes closed, both hands clenched at her sides.

He experienced a moment of unreasonable fright before he saw that she was breathing. He went out quietly.

Laura was waiting out at the curb when Steve drove up. Her face was drawn and she had the morning *Times* under her arm.

As she got into the car, she said, "I've had the acid test. I have never in my life wanted a drink more. But I didn't take it."

"Good girl," Steve said warmly. "Let's not think about it. It's really Harry Bergdahl's headache, isn't it? It's none of our business."

Her voice was tight. "It's not our business that a man is dead? After what I told you? We should have talked to Jameson."

"I did," Steve told her. "Last night. And I'm sure he had no intention of rolling his car over that cliff. I'm sure I convinced him he should show up for the picture."

Steve had to keep his eyes on the traffic but he could sense that Laura was staring at him. Finally she whispered, "Steve, could it have been murder?"

He nodded. "Two men from Homicide were over to my house last night. Incidentally, I didn't tell them about that rumor you told me. And you had better forget it."

"Why . . . ? If it isn't murder, why?"

"Because if it wasn't murder, the insurance company could still claim collusion. And then there might not be a picture."

Silence. He came to a break in the traffic and stole a glance at Laura. She was staring straight ahead, her face rigid.

42

"We're not the police," Steve reminded her gently. "And Hart Jameson is dead. *Nothing* can bring him back."

Laura was silent for blocks. And then she said hoarsely, "I wish I weren't so goddamned broke!"

It was a bad day. Laura was jittery and the others were wooden. It was a day of almost completely wasted film. Steve fought his irritation and tried to think of nothing but the picture. He was not successful. He was a man with a conscience.

Laura had voiced a rumor and Jameson had verified it. And he had withheld that information from the police. No matter how he tried to rationalize it, that had been morally, if not legally, wrong. Dave Sidney had argued in support of his silence, but Dave had admitted he took a light view of the morality of money.

Involved financial manipulations had always been an accepted part of the picture business. Since the advent of confiscatory income taxes, those manipulations had ventured farther and farther from the true intent of the Federal law. So far as he knew, however, they had never before ventured into the realm of murder.

He told himself that he couldn't be sure it was murder. The police would decide that. They had experts whose job it was to decide that definitely. And if they should discover it wasn't murder, there would be no moral problem for him to solve.

The script girl rode home with them. He and Laura carefully avoided any discussion of Hart Jameson's death.

44

He dropped Laura first, and told her, "It was a bad day. Tomorrow will be better."

She patted his hand. "I was abominable. It won't happen again, I promise you."

As they drove on, the script girl said, "I wonder who'll take Hart Jameson's part? He's going to be difficult to replace, isn't he?"

"Very," Steve agreed. "Mr. Bergdahl is working on that now."

And what else, he wondered, was Mr. Bergdahl working on now? On his alibi perhaps? He hadn't seen a paper since this morning's *Times*. By now the wet-eyed cinema columnists had undoubtedly taken over and the public would be deluged with another tidal wave of bathos. The "exciting newcomer" was dead, dead, dead.

A cerise Cadillac convertible was parked in his driveway, and he tried to remember which of his or Marcia's friends drove a car like that.

It was Harry's car. He was sitting out on the sundeck, a drink in his hand. Marcia sat nearby in a terrycloth robe over her swim suit.

Steve went over to kiss her and she turned her cheek.

Harry said, "Some kiss. If Dotty tried that, I'd throw her into the pool."

Steve took a deep breath and turned to face Bergdahl. "I suppose the columnists are pulling all the stops."

Bergdahl shrugged. "I only read the financial page. I can get Leslie for the lead. I can get him pretty cheap, too. Okay?"

"Fine," Steve said. "I wasted your money today, Harry."

Bergdahl shrugged again. "That figured. Did Laura show up sober?"

Steve nodded and went over to mix a drink. With

his back to Harry, he asked, "Has Sergeant Morrow been around?"

"No. There's a real nasty slob nosing around for the insurance company, though. Polack bastard named Tomkevic. He's got a nasty mind, Steve. Keep your temper under control."

Steve turned to find Harry looking at him meaningfully. He said, "I haven't any temper left. I didn't even have the gumption to horsewhip that cast today."

"It's the first bad day," Harry said soothingly. "Don't fret, Steve." He looked at Marcia and away. He sipped his drink.

Marcia murmured, "Excuse *me!*" She rose and went down the steps to the pool.

Harry inclined his head. "What's with her?"

"I guess she's annoyed with me. She thinks I'm keeping some deep, dark secret from her."

"Are you?"

Steve shook his head.

Harry said quietly, "Dave told me about the talk you had with Jameson. Did you tell Marcia about that, too?"

Steve shook his head again.

"Smart boy," Harry said. "Women—they can't keep nothing to themselves."

Steve sipped his drink.

Harry finished his and expelled his breath. He stared at Steve steadily. "For Christ's sake, you don't think I killed him, do you?"

Steve said evenly, "Of course not. It was an accident, wasn't it? Have the police decided?"

"I think they're willing to write it off as an accident, but that Polack Tomkevic sure as hell ain't about to. You watch out for him, Steve."

"I'll be careful," Steve promised. "Will Leslie be ready tomorrow?"

"I'll have him there." Harry stood up. "And Dave will ride with you." He studied Steve thoughtfully. "Have you ever decided who your real friends are, Steve?"

Steve smiled. "Mmmm-hmmm. People who don't interfere."

He went to the door with Harry and then came to watch Marcia splashing in the pool. She was blithely ignoring him. He started down the steps to the pool when the housekeeper came out to tell him a Mr. Tomkevic was waiting to see him.

The pressure mounted in Steve's chest. He said, "I'll see him out here."

He was mixing a drink when the brown-eyed, soft-voiced man came out to the sundeck.

Steve indicated a chair and asked, "Drink, Mr. Tomkevic?"

"No, thanks. My first trip here doesn't seem quite as silly now as it did to you then, does it?"

Steve shrugged.

Tomkevic sat down and stared at Steve. Then, "I suppose you're about to have dinner. I'll try to be brief."

He went on then, to explain about the accident. Jameson's car had gone over the bluff from an empty lot, and it had to bump across an extremely rough stretch of ground in order to reach the edge from which it fell.

"He was probably drunk," Steve explained.

"It's been established that he'd been drinking. And drunken drivers have accidents. But not accidents like this. It would have required a rather high degree of rationality simply to keep the engine running across that field. You must remember there was no automatic transmission in that car, and that field could not be traversed in high gear."

47

Steve asked quietly, "Why are you telling me this, Mr. Tomkevic? I'm not a detective."

Tomkevic said blandly, "Everything I've learned about you today indicates you're a man of exceptional integrity, Mr. Leander. I want you to reëxamine your conversation with Hart Jameson and determine if there isn't something you overlooked."

"I'm not following you," Steve said.

Tomkevic frowned and leaned forward. "Frankly, I'm checking a rumor. The rumor is that Jameson never had any idea of appearing in this picture, for which he was insured."

Steve could feel the pulse beat in his wrist. He looked down at the pool. Marcia had taken off her swimming cap and was drying herself.

"Well . . . ?" Tomkevic prompted.

Steve said easily, "You hear a lot of damn-fool rumors in this business, Mr. Tomkevic. Jameson was signed to play and he would have been in legal hot water if he hadn't."

"Perhaps. Are you telling me now that you and Jameson didn't discuss his appearance in the picture?"

"I'm not obligated to tell you anything, am I?"

"That would depend on your conscience, Mr. Leander. A man is dead. Anything you can tell me that would help to uncover the reason for his death is important. Don't you agree with that?"

"I agree with that. But I don't believe any other conversation we may have had about the picture is anybody's business but mine."

Tomkevic's face tightened. "Well, you've told me enough to confirm my suspicion. I'm sure you'll realize later that honesty is your only sensible course."

Steve flushed. He asked, "Confirm *what* suspicion?"

"That Jameson's death was no accident."

"Isn't that a question for the police to decide?"

48

Tomkevic said wearily, "The police are overloaded. Even for a death as headline-worthy as this one, their time is limited. Mine isn't, and they'll ride with me."

"But will the courts?"

Tomkevic stood up. "Mr. Leander, I think I can safely say that by the time this mess gets into a court, it will be a *criminal* court. And the state will be the plaintiff."

Steve's flush deepened. "Is that an accusation?"

Tomkevic met his glare. "At the moment, I can only accuse you of a serious error in judgment. I am going to get to the truth of this accident. You would have done *both* of us a service if you had been completely coöperative with me today."

Steve said nothing.

Tomkevic said, "It still isn't too late."

"I'm sure you can find your way out," Steve told him.

Tomkevic smiled bitterly. He glanced past Steve to where Marcia was coming slowly up the steps. Then he turned abruptly and left.

Marcia went past to the portable bar and began to mix a drink.

"And why are you sulking?" Steve asked.

She kept her back to him. "I'm not. Who was that man?"

"An insurance investigator."

She turned around. "If this marriage means as much to you as it does to me, I think I've a right to know what you and Dave were talking about last night."

"We were talking about Hart Jameson. There's a suspicion afloat that he may have been murdered. Now, do you think either Dave or I could murder?"

"No. But I do think you know something about Jameson's death that you're not telling me. Or the police." She inhaled heavily. "And I think you've made a very bad moral decision."

49

"Only the nonparticipants," he said, "can afford this flawless morality."

Her voice was high. "Now what in hell did that mean? How am I a nonparticipant in anything that happens to you?"

"You're a nonparticipant in the frightened, scrambling, conniving world I work in. That's what I meant."

"I see. And you've decided to be a frightened, scrambling conniver. Is that it?"

He held his tongue for seconds and then said quietly, "You didn't mean that."

"They were your words," she answered. "Steve, this picture has become so important to you, you're letting Harry Bergdahl destroy you."

"That is absurd," he said. "Harry hasn't interfered once. I'm shooting this picture exactly the way I want to." He finished his drink. "And making the best picture I'm capable of is the only kind of morality I'm concerned about."

"Oh, God . . . !" she said. "Do you realize how pretentious you just sounded?"

"You tell me," he answered evenly. "You're good at it."

She glared, and tears came to her eyes. She set her untasted drink on a table and walked quickly into the house.

He sat there, trying to blank his mind. He couldn't get emotionally involved in a domestic crisis now. He needed every ounce of energy and serenity he could find to make this picture successful.

He was eating dinner alone when Marcia went out. He called after her and though he knew she had heard him, she didn't pause. The front door slammed with a force that shook the floor.

He finished his meal and took the percolator of coffee with him into the study. He was well into the script when the phone rang.

He picked it up and a doubtful masculine voice asked, "Mr. Leander?"

"Yes."

A pause, and then hesitantly, "This is a—a friend of a friend of Hart Jameson's. I wonder if I could see you tonight?"

"I'm very busy," Steve said. "Could I have your name, please?"

"Not unless I can see you," the man said. "This friend of Jameson's that I know, she was—over at his apartment last night."

Steve said steadily, "The police are looking for her. If she's a friend of yours, you'd be doing her a service by advising her to report to the nearest police station."

"She doesn't want to. She's innocent, see? But she doesn't want any part of the police."

"If she's innocent, why not?"

The man's voice was lower now and slightly shaky. "Well, it would just cause a lot of trouble. She heard something she wasn't supposed to hear, I guess, and she doesn't want to cause anybody any trouble."

The pressure was building up again in Steve's chest. He took a deep breath. "Why do you want to see me?"

"I'm an actor. I thought you might have a little something for me in this picture you're shooting."

"I see. How did you get my phone number?"

"Hart Jameson had it, and my friend got it from him."

"He had Mr. Bergdahl's number, too. He's the producer. Why didn't you phone him?"

"To tell you the truth, Mr. Leander, because I'm scared to death of Harry Bergdahl."

"But not of the police? Do you realize you're withholding information from them by not telling them the name of the girl?"

"I'm going to protect her. I wouldn't want her to get on the wrong side of Harry Bergdahl, not in this town."

"Oh . . . ? She's an actress, is she?"

"She likes to call herself one." A pause. "Am I wasting your time, Mr. Leander?"

"I'm not sure what you're doing," Steve said frankly. "And I'm also not sure why I'm listening. Why don't you want to give me your name?"

There was a silence that lasted for seconds. And then the man asked, "Did you see *Dim Thunder?*"

"Yes."

"Do you remember that bar scene, where the drunk went loco?"

"I most certainly do."

"I played that drunk. My name is Mitchell Morton. I wouldn't ask for a part any bigger than that."

Steve stared at his desk top and then at the script. Finally he said, "There's a part that small and that good in this picture. Why don't you come over here and we'll talk about it?"

After he had hung up, he went over to the bookcase and pulled two books from a shelf. There was a .32 there which he kept because the house was so isolated.

After a few moments, he replaced the books without touching the gun. What did he have to fear from an actor?

SEVEN

Had he been blackmailed? Not yet, of course. He had not promised Morton a part. He had agreed to talk with him about it but he had promised nothing. He went out onto the front lawn to wait.

The santana was blowing, and the evening was unusually warm and dry. To his right the shoreline of Santa Monica Bay was clear from Point Dume to Palos Verdes.

He hadn't come out to enjoy the view. He kept his eyes on the glistening traffic of Sunset Boulevard, far below.

A car turned off from the artery, and he felt a flutter in his stomach. It turned again at a driveway halfway up the hill. He waited.

Now, another car turned off from the main road, and this one was coming all the way up. He went out to the curb to wait. It was a three-year-old, two-door Plymouth sedan.

He had seen Mitchell Morton only in that memorable bit in *Dim Thunder*, but he recognized him as he stepped from the car.

He had a brush haircut and impressive shoulders. He was young and his youth was apparent in the present situation. Steve sensed that beneath the true actor's

53

cultivated poise, young Morton was uncertain and frightened.

He came over to stand squarely in front of Steve and he managed to smile. "Call me a son-of-a-bitch and send me packing. I'm sure that's what I deserve."

Some of Steve's apprehension disappeared, and his own poise returned. He smiled. "Nobody's perfect. I'm not sure whether I'm being blackmailed or not. I've been trying to decide."

"It's certainly not blackmail," Morton said quietly. "My friend isn't about to go to the police, no matter what happens to the career of Mitchell Morton." His chin lifted. "I used that line so you wouldn't hang up on me. Slimy, right?"

Steve shrugged. "You're in a rough profession."

They stood silently a moment. *He's scared,* Steve thought. *He's young and desperate and gutty, but he's scared.*

It was growing dark now, and the lights were beginning to dot the hills. Steve said, "You must be very hungry and you're only asking for a crumb. Come on into the house. I have an extra copy of the script I can give you."

Morton made no move. He said hoarsely, "Why don't you tell me to beat it?"

"Forget how you got here," Steve advised him gently. "You're something new, an actor with a conscience. Come on."

In Steve's study they talked for about ten minutes, and Steve learned that Mitchell Morton had studied with Jameson in New York. They hadn't been exactly friends, Morton was quick to explain, but when he had come out here, Jameson's had been the only familiar face.

"And through Jameson you met this girl?"

54

Morton said, "I'd rather not talk about the girl, Mr. Leander."

"I'd like to, a little. For instance, can you be sure she's not connected with Jameson's death in some way?"

"I'm positive," Morton answered.

"And you weren't, by any chance, the unidentified man who was seen in the area on top of the bluff there, were you?"

Morton shook his head. "I don't know anything about him and neither does my friend. I asked her about that when I read it in the paper."

Steve looked at the young man levelly. "Do you think Jameson's death was an accident?"

Morton nodded.

Steve smiled. "It's easier to lie with a nod than with words, isn't it? You don't really think his death was an accident."

"Maybe not. But I swear to you that I don't know it was anything else."

Steve stood up and handed Morton the script. "Okay. I'll tell Mr. Bergdahl you've been promised that bit. Phone me the early part of next week. We'll probably shoot that Thursday or Friday."

"Thank you," Morton said warmly. "Thank you for treating me better than I deserve."

It was, Steve reflected, the first time in his life he had been accused of that. He went out to the car with Morton and stood there long after Morton was out of sight, hoping that another car would turn up from the road. Where could Marcia have gone? To John Abbot?

She was being unreasonable, but that was a failing of her sex. He had worked with enough temperamental women to be able to cope with their absurdities. With Marcia, because of the emotional attachment, it was more difficult. But she'd come back to reason eventually, he assured himself.

He phoned Bergdahl and found him at home. He said, "I promised a lad named Mitchell Morton a piece in that lake cottage scene. Know him?"

"The name only . . . Wait, did I see it on a list? Was he listed in *Red Channels?*"

"I have no idea," Steve answered.

"Or did some broad mention his name? It sticks in my mind, for some reason."

"If you saw *Dim Thunder,* he played that pathological bit in the bar scene."

"I didn't see it," Harry said. "Well, I'll check; I've got all the lists. That Tomkevic was here right after dinner. The son-of-a-bitch is going to wind up with a bloody nose if he don't get out of my hair."

Steve said nothing.

"I talked to Sergeant Morrow," Harry went on, "and the law's about convinced it was an accident. So what's bothering the Polack? Jesus, it ain't *his* money!"

"He'll give up after a while," Steve said soothingly. "Remember your ulcer, Harry."

"Yeh, yeh. Mitchell Morton, Mitchell Morton—damn it, I'll bet he's a Commie."

"Check it," Steve said. "Is Dave coming over here in the morning or does he want me to pick him up?"

"He'll come there. Look, we're planning a cast party for Saturday night. You and Marcia going to be free?"

"I'm sure we are. I'll let you know. Marcia's not home right now."

Harry chuckled. "If she's out on the town, tell me where. That's some doll you got, mister."

"Thank you. I'll tell her you said that. I'll *warn* her. Now don't fret, Harry. Everything is going to work out well."

Bergdahl chuckled again. "That's a switch, *you* telling *me* not to fret. Be seein' you, kid."

Steve went back to the script, searching for soft spots he could discuss with Dave Sidney tomorrow.

At eleven he went out to the front again, and it was still warm for a California night. He stayed out until midnight, looking at the lights and waiting for Marcia. Finally he went in and to bed. He was asleep when she came home.

In the morning *Times* he read that an autopsy had discovered nothing beyond an exorbitant amount of alcohol in the body of Hart Jameson. The police, however, were still not ready to write off the death as accidental. No reason was given for this attitude, but Steve could guess that a man named Tomkevic might be mainly responsible for it.

The signing of Tom Leslie for Jameson's part was given a fat two paragraphs in Hedda's column, and the local columnist gave that and the Jameson tragedy his entire column. Harry would be happy about the free ink.

Steve was drinking his coffee when Dave Sidney came. Dave looked haggard.

"Sit down and have some coffee," Steve suggested. "Hung over?"

Dave shook his head as he sat down at the far end of the table from Steve. "I've been playing amateur detective. I was up until three this morning."

"Now, Dave, what can you learn that a police department and a private detective can't?"

"Well, to begin with, I know a couple of Hart's girl friends. To my mind, that floozie who was with Hart Wednesday night could be the big key."

"I'll know her if I ever meet her," Steve said. "That is, unless she changes her brand of perfume. I'll never forget that odor."

"It could be a common perfume," Dave suggested.

Steve shook his head. "I've worked with women at all income levels, and I never smelled anything like this before." He poured Dave a cup of coffee. "Run into my study and get the script, will you? There are some shots I've marked for sharpening."

It was the start of a rewarding day. Tom Leslie, unlike Jameson, was a trained and disciplined talent. He would be another plus for the picture. And Laura moved through her scenes with competence and grace. There were moments when she seemed almost like an actress.

At the first break, Dave Sidney told Steve, "I don't know what's happening, but it's coming alive, isn't it?"

Steve nodded and smiled. "To tell you the truth, I'm not sure what's happening either, but I think this Leslie is a boy who pulls the best out of all the others."

There was a silence and Steve wondered if his shameful, fleeting thought had been shared by Dave. The death of Hart Jameson had not been a completely ill wind.

Dave said quietly, "I hope Uncle Harry gets the rest of his money."

Steve said confidently, "With stuff like this to show angels, he's got sound collateral." And he reflected that neither of them had used the word "insurance."

Laura got a ride home with Leslie that evening. Steve and Dave were the only occupants of Steve's car. Dave dozed as they drove along the Coast Highway, and Steve thought back on the day with satisfaction.

This picture had to be finished. Harry would have to get the money any damned way he could. This picture had to be done right. There were some expenses ahead. There were some sets they couldn't cheat on without damaging the picture.

Dave mumbled something and Steve glanced his way, but Dave's eyes were closed. This picture could do a lot for Dave's reputation, and Dave was Harry's nephew. This picture would be financed. Harry would see to that.

As he got out of the car in Steve's driveway, Dave asked, "Are you and Marcia going to the party tomorrow night?"

"Probably," Steve answered. "Though I can't vouch for Marcia. She's not talking to me."

"She's not still angry because of Wednesday night, is she? I mean—when you and I talked outside?"

Steve nodded. "I'll probably go, either way. I could use a real Bergdahl wingding about now."

"Don't forget the funeral is tomorrow," Dave reminded him. "Uncle Harry would like to see us all there."

"I'd forgotten," Steve said slowly. "Yes, we'd better all go."

It wasn't anything he was looking forward to, and he was sure Harry wanted them there only for the promotional effect. But it was no time to flaunt tradition.

And the party—he hoped Marcia would agree to go. A Bergdahl party would do them both a lot of good. If they drank enough.

Marcia wasn't home. She had left a note: "I decided to spend a long week end with the children. I'll be home Monday."

In the kitchen the housekeeper told him, "Mrs. Leander won't be home until Monday. Did you get her note?"

Steve nodded.

The woman hesitated. Then, "Is there something wrong, Mr. Leander? I know it's none of my business, but you two always got along so fine . . ." Her voice trailed off and she looked uncomfortable.

"There's nothing wrong, Mrs. Burke," Steve said placidly. "She simply went up to camp to see the children." He smiled. "I think I'll eat at the club tonight.

That way you can make the early movie at the Bay."

He felt lethargic after his shower. He lay on the bed in his robe and tried to nap. Usually he could doze off in a few minutes, but not tonight.

Both John Abbot and Laura had warned him against Harry Bergdahl, and they were a pair of old pros. Of course, neither of them had been proved right so far. He had had no interference from Harry on the picture, and he would not have been involved in the death of Hart Jameson if he hadn't listened to Laura's gossip. And he wouldn't have been in a position to listen to Laura's gossip if she hadn't begged him for a part in the picture.

No, that wasn't fair. He had gone to see Jameson of his own volition, and he had lied to the police about the conversation they had had. He couldn't blame Laura for any of that. If Harry Bergdahl was not a murderer, what harm had been done by his lie? A lie is a lie is a lie . . .

He thought of Marcia, and desire swelled in him. He got up irritatedly and dressed.

In the grill of the Canyon Country Club, Dow Allen and Jack Delahunt waved to him from a table overlooking the eighteenth green. Steve went over.

Dow said, "You have the look of a man with a free evening. How about some poker?"

Steve sat down. "Maybe. My wife's out of town for the week end."

"Great," Dow said. "That was too bad about Jameson. Harry was ready, though, wasn't he?"

Jack laughed and Steve looked between them grimly. "I hope that was a gag, though it was a bad one. Am I getting that kind of reputation?"

Dow smiled. "Not you, buddy. Harry's always had that kind of reputation."

"As a murderer? Not *quite*."

Jack said seriously, "As anything he needs to be to stay in business. I wouldn't put murder past him, Steve."

"Nonsense," Steve said angrily. "Let's talk about something else."

"Let's talk about the picture," Allen said genially. "The word is you've got a winner. And now you come up smelling like roses with Tom Leslie."

"And Laura Spain," Delahunt added. "How did you ever convince her it was time to act her age?"

"Laura and I are old friends," Steve said.

"Is she off the soup?" Dow asked.

Steve nodded and picked up a menu. "Laura is doing very well. She's a real pro."

Dow laughed. "You sounded smug, kid."

"Why not?" Jack put in. "He's working, isn't he?"

They all had dinner in the grill, and then some others came and they went into the card room.

It was a table stakes game, and the cards were kind to Steve. He didn't concentrate properly and completely misplayed the best hand he was dealt all evening.

Despite this, when they broke up at three o'clock, he was an even four hundred dollars ahead for the session.

Dow Allen said, "You're the luckiest and lousiest poker player in the world. Kid, you stink."

"I'm not usually this bad," Steve answered. "I just couldn't get my mind on the cards."

"I'll vouch for that," Delahunt said. "Next to Harry Bergdahl, I think Steve is the best poker player I know." He smiled. "I would have loved to have been there when you two talked terms."

"My agent did that," Steve said. "I wouldn't dare to cross swords with Harry Bergdahl."

EIGHT

Sylvan Glade advertised quite honestly that it took the burden of decision from the bereaved relatives of the departed. It had its own interdenominational chapel, crypts, mausoleum, crematorium, casket salesroom, limousines, ushers, social secretary, publicity department and grave-digging machine with skilled operator. And photogenic professional mourners, if required.

It also had fountains, statuary, gigantic murals, wide winding drives and everything else that could contribute to the general bad taste of a town that specialized in bad taste. As one of the directors had boasted in an alcoholic moment, "We put on one hell of a show. But Jesus, a man only dies once!"

A package deal, Steve thought, in the terminology of his trade. He and Laura were driving in his car through the gaping teen-agers and sagging housewives who lined the green macadam drive that led to the chapel parking lot.

"Where's the ringmaster?" Laura asked. "God . . . !"

"Easy, girl. This is nothing, compared with Valentino's funeral."

"You don't remember that," Laura answered. "That was before your time. And mine, too."

Steve smiled. "It was before *mine,* at any rate. There were giants in those days."

Laura shook her head. "There was a sucker audience. . . . I'm a lousy actress, aren't I, Steve?"

"No," he said firmly. "Because you were a star, you never had to learn to act. But you were great yesterday. This picture could start a whole new career for you, Laura."

"An acting career," she said musingly. "Well, that would be a change."

They both laughed, and then Laura said, "Heavens, what will all these cretins think? We had better look sad."

Harry Bergdahl looked sad. He sat in the second row with a handkerchief in his hand, occasionally dabbing at his eyes.

"Smog?" Laura whispered to Steve. "I didn't notice it."

"Shut up," Steve whispered. "I suppose we'd better go up to view the body?"

"You go," Laura said. "I never could do that."

It was going to be a full house. As he returned to sit next to Laura, Steve saw Tomkevic in one of the back rows near the entrance. Mitchell Morton was in a front row. He was apparently one of the pallbearers. Dave Sidney sat next to his uncle, his face perfectly blank, almost bored. From the other side of Harry, Dotty smiled timidly at Steve. In one of the corners a flash bulb flared.

Were these casual onlookers representative of the mourners? Steve saw no genuine tears. Hadn't Jameson any family? He felt a cold sickness growing in him as he took his seat.

Laura sat rigidly, staring at the neck of the man ahead, while the cleric supplied by the management spoke unctuously of "this untimely departure of a young and brilliant talent."

There were a few wet eyes when he had finished. In

the sixth row a chunky teen-ager sobbed noisily. Steve thought of the waiting kids lining the macadam drive outside and he asked Laura, "Should we go to the grave with the procession?"

"No," she said. "We put in an appearance. Harry can't have any complaints if we don't contribute further to this—circus."

Steve frowned, hesitating.

Laura said, *"Please,* Steve . . . ? I don't like funerals. I think they're vulgar."

"All right," he said soothingly. "Let the others get ahead of us and we'll go directly to the parking lot."

The parking lot was almost deserted when he and Laura walked over to his car some minutes later. There was a green Pontiac parked two stalls away.

Tomkevic stepped from the Pontiac as Steve opened the door for Laura.

He asked in his soft voice, "Could I have a minute, Mr. Leander?"

Steve closed the door and turned to face the investigator. "Yes . . . ?"

Tomkevic said, "I understand Mitchell Morton is going to have a part in your picture?"

"A small part," Steve agreed.

"Did you hire him, or Mr. Bergdahl?"

"I talked with Mr. Morton. No contract has been signed. Is there some reason why I shouldn't hire him?"

"None that I know of. I simply wanted to learn who had hired him. He hasn't worked in any of your other pictures, has he?"

"No."

"You knew him personally, did you, before casting him?"

Steve shook his head.

Tomkevic frowned. "Mr. Bergdahl did. I'm surprised he didn't go to Mr. Bergdahl."

Steve said nothing.

"Aren't you?" Tomkevic asked quietly.

"Not particularly. Anything else, Mr. Tomkevic?"

The investigator's eyes hardened. "Yes. Do you think you need to be as frightened and secretive as you are? You have a sound reputation in this town." He paused. "Or *had*."

Steve said heatedly, "Don't be insolent. You're not heavy enough to carry it off."

The investigator smiled. "I'm not too big, I'll admit. But then, I'm not frightened, either. I'll see you again, Mr. Leander."

"I'm not looking forward to it," Steve said, and went around the car to the driver's side.

Laura said, "Well! And what was all that about?"

"I've no idea," Steve said angrily. "He's an investigator for the company that insured Jameson."

"I thought this morning's paper said the police had decided it was an accident?"

"There's absolutely no reason in the world," Steve said, "to consider it anything else. Let's not see any more goblins, Laura. We went through that phase."

She sighed and said nothing. She said nothing for the rest of the trip. As Steve dropped her he said, "I'll see you at the party tonight."

"I'm not sure I'm going," she answered. "I hate to sit around and watch everybody drink. Do you think Harry would mind very much if I didn't come?"

Steve shrugged.

"Is Marcia going?"

"She's out of town. She went up to the kids' camp."

A moment's silence, and then Laura said, "I suppose it would be good politics to go. Don't worry about me; I'll get there all right. I'll want to leave early."

Steve went home to his big and empty house. The parking-lot dialogue with Tomkevic had unsettled him

65

again. And Tomkevic's claim that Harry had known Morton was a disturbing item. Harry had made too much of a point of his *not* knowing Mitchell Morton.

Damn it, Jameson was dead. Dead and now buried. And the police had decided it was an accident. They were the official arbiters.

He lay on the couch in his study and thought of Marcia, and desire grew in him again and his irritation deepened. She had never earned a dime in her life. She had no idea of the savage and incessant competition in the industry. Her duty was to sustain him, not to judge him.

It had been two weeks since their matinée session and he was no benedict and she was well aware of that. She was not exactly frigid herself.

He put on his trunks and went down to the pool. He dived, he swam, he lolled in the sun. He tried to forget Jameson and Morton and Tomkevic and Bergdahl. But the thought of Marcia stayed with him.

At five o'clock Harry phoned. "Dave tells me Marcia's out of town?"

"That's right, Harry. But I'll be there, bright and sober."

"Maybe I should invite something special for you? About eighteen or nineteen, something stacked?"

"I wouldn't know what to do with one like that. I'm sorry I didn't—go to the grave, Harry, but funerals give me the creeps."

"Oh . . . ? I thought maybe it was Laura that didn't want to go."

"No," Steve lied, "it was my idea. Tomkevic was waiting for me on the chapel parking lot. He won't give up, will he?"

"He don't scare me," Harry said. "Well, there'll be a lot of broads here, kid, so don't drink too much."

"I'll be careful. See you, Harry."

"Wait . . ." Bergdahl said. "That Mitchell Morton —he's okay, he's clean. I checked him."

"Glad to hear it," Steve said. "He'll be another small plus for the picture."

How did Dave know that Marcia was out of town? He had left him at the front door yesterday and not talked to him since. And when they had parted, even Steve hadn't known Marcia wasn't home.

Perhaps Dave had learned it from Laura. Or perhaps his amateur detective work had extended into the private life of the Leanders.

The rear patio was lighted by gay Japanese lanterns, and the concrete badminton court had been waxed for dancing. The bar was built-in near the huge, used-brick fireplace. Small wrought-iron and glass tables were set back around the wide deck of the pool.

Next to Steve at the bar, Mitchell Morton said, "Simple suburban living. I wonder if I'll ever make it."

Steve laughed. "Not unless you can get into a position to use a capital-gains gimmick. Not on salary alone, not any more."

From the other side of Morton, the girl he had brought said, "Okay, Mitch, don't I meet the important people, too?"

She was a thin girl with her black hair in a Hollywood version of a Dutch cut. Her voice was low and pleasant.

Morton performed the introduction and then Dotty Bergdahl came over to tell him coyly that there were "oodles of people just gasping to meet Steven Leander."

He met four of the oodles, three women and one man, and then Dotty led him to the badminton court, where Tom Leslie was dancing with a spectacular blonde.

"I want to talk to you," she explained, "and I don't

want Harry to think I'm pumping you. Let's dance."

Steve frowned. "Pumping me . . . ? About what?"

"About a rumor I heard, that Jameson was *planning* to have an accident in his car."

"Dotty, in this business we hear ridiculous rumors every day." He moved her along the edge of the court, aware of her fine body, of her firm breasts tight against his chest.

"I know that," she admitted. "But what is Harry so nervous about? Why is that insurance detective bothering him all the time?"

"I have no idea."

"He's been going out practically every night. Why?"

Steve smiled sadly. "Honey, how in hell would I know?"

"Men . . . !" she said. "And you and Marcia had a fight, too, didn't you? And there's some big, mysterious secret about that."

"She went up to see the kids. Marcia and I have fought before, Dotty. We're not newlyweds."

She looked up at him beseechingly. "I know there's something horrible going on, Steve. Why don't you tell me what it is?"

He said gravely, "If there's anything horrible going on, I swear to you, Dotty, that I don't know what it is. Horrible things are going on in this town every minute."

"Not things Harry's involved in." She took a deep breath. "I know what you think of me—a peroxide nitwit. But I've been good for Harry. I brought these young people around, and he's put out some pictures with vitality and youth in them. If he's in trouble, don't be too sure I can't help him."

"Dotty, I never thought of you as a peroxide nitwit. I can't seem to think of you as anything but about the

68

most seductive female in the county. And if Harry's in trouble, he hasn't told me about it."

She moved closer and desire quickened in Steve. She asked softly, "Is it about Hart Jameson?" Her voice was even quieter. "Or is it a girl? Tell me, please, Steve."

"I don't know. So help me, honey, I don't know. You're closer to him than I am. He'd tell you things he wouldn't tell me."

"Not if it's about a girl," she insisted. "And I think it is."

Steve didn't have time to answer. A genial voice at his elbow said loudly, "Get one of your own, Leander. This one's mine."

Steve smiled and relinquished Dotty Bergdahl to her leering husband.

He went back to the bar. Morton's black-haired girl friend was talking with Dave Sidney there. Morton was at one of the tables, talking with Laura Spain and the dialogue director.

Dave said, "Jean thinks you dance very well for an older man."

The girl grimaced. "I didn't say anything about an *older* man. Dave's trying to blight my career."

"Don't butter him," Dave said. "He's the last local bastion of integrity." He looked around the yard. "I wonder where my giddy companion has disappeared to?"

Jean yawned. "You could check the bedrooms and the bushes. That one belongs on a leash."

Steve asked the bartender for a Scotch and water and turned to watch Harry dancing with Dotty. Harry was talking to her very earnestly, and Dotty's face looked grim and stubborn.

The conversational murmur was higher now and

69

more people were coming in. Dave said, "I love Uncle Harry's idea of a *cast* party. He means the casts of all his pictures and all the people they ever met."

Above the swaying lanterns the stars were clear and the moon full. Steve drank slowly and thought of Marcia.

Dave said, "Ah, here comes my lovely now."

Jean said, "She's looking petulant. Somebody must have said no to her."

Steve saw a girl in a white sheath dress coming toward them, walking carefully, as though on the edge of drunken oblivion. Her full breasts were almost emerging from the top of the tight dress, and its tautness emphasized the functional, rounded beauty of her behind. She had large brown eyes and a sulky, full-lipped mouth and a tangle of dark brown hair. Dave had brought a tigress.

Then Laura beckoned to him and he went over to her table. As he sat down she said, "I'm here to keep you out of the clutches of females like that one you were ogling. It's the least I can do for your absent and mistreated wife."

Steve smiled. "All woman, isn't she? I had no idea Dave was that virile."

Morton smiled. Laura said, "I had no idea *you* were. Heavens, the way you were *leering* at her . . ."

"My party look," Steve explained. "She probably considers me a licentious old man."

Laura raised her eyebrows. "Old . . . ?"

Morton said, "Not her, not Pat Cullum. The adolescents can't afford her."

"An actress?" Steve asked.

"She likes to think she is," Morton answered.

It was almost the same phrase he had used about his friend, the night he had phoned Steve. Steve looked at him searchingly now.

Morton met his gaze and said, "I use that expression too much. I suppose it's because of envy. I really only know the girl by hearsay."

Laura stared at her admiringly and murmured, "I often wonder how far I could have gone with a larger cup size."

Steve laughed and rose. "Why don't we dance, Laura, and dream of better days?"

She sighed. "What a romantic approach! Let's go, gallant."

They had danced together before and discovered they were well suited, and they enjoyed it now. The music was continuous, fed to the yard through speakers from a record player in the house.

They had danced without speaking for perhaps three minutes when Laura said, "I think the young actors coming up are more serious than they used to be."

"Morton, do you mean?"

"For one. And Tom Leslie for another. They're more thoughtful, more analytical about their profession."

"And less colorful," Steve added. "Though they're certainly easier to work with, except for the sweat-shirt gang."

"If we ever come into the age of reason in this business," Laura asked, "what's going to happen to men like Harry Bergdahl?"

"In any age, men like Harry are going to survive, Laura. They're adaptable. Harry's not stupid."

"No. That's right." She sighed. "I keep thinking of him as a murderer. But he wouldn't be that stupid, would he?"

Steve didn't answer. Dave Sidney went by, dancing with Pat Cullum, and the girl didn't look drunk now, flawlessly following the intricate pattern of Dave's steps.

"I wish I were twenty-four," Steve said.

Laura chuckled. "I'd settle for thirty-four. But you're that now, aren't you?"

"Thirty-seven," Steve answered, "but tonight I mean to howl."

"Not I," Laura said. "A funeral and an orgy in the same day are too much for me. I've made my token appearance at both shows and I'm ready for my hot Ovaltine." She grimaced. "I need all my strength for my new career."

She left soon after that and Steve went to the bar again. Harry was there, talking with the black-haired Jean. Though the night was cool, Harry's forehead and neck were wet with perspiration and his tongue was thick.

He put a heavy hand on Steve's shoulder. "Met Jean yet, kid?"

Steve nodded. "Dave introduced us. She's too young for us, Harry."

Bergdahl said heavily, "She's two years younger than my wife. Speak for yourself, sissy." He laughed, and said to the girl, "I leave you in safe hands." He swaggered away.

Jean exhaled audibly. "What do I say? Not what I'm thinking, or I go back to typing for a living."

"Smile and look tolerant," Steve advised her. "Self-discipline, that's the virtue. Control, control, control . . ."

"Isn't there," she asked, "some *vertical* way to get ahead in this business?"

"There are a number of ways," Steve said. "Some of them vertical. I think the best way is to be stubborn and disciplined." He asked the bartender for a Scotch and water.

"Wouldn't talent help?" Jean asked, as he turned back to her.

"Always. But there's damned little of it around. You stick with that Morton boy. He's going up."

"I don't want to ride anybody," she said firmly, "and I want to decide who rides me. If you'll pardon the vulgarism, which I'm sure you will. In New York, talent was very important. I should have stayed there."

"And why didn't you?"

"Because everything is moving out here."

"Including Mitchell Morton?"

She shook her head. "Mitch is about the best friend I have. But we don't ring any bells in each other. I wish we did. He's a damned saint."

Then Dave was coming over with his tigress, and Steve was introduced. And as the girl moved closer, to face the bar, Steve smelled the fragrance he couldn't forget, the perfume he had first smelled in Hart Jameson's apartment.

He said a little shakily, "I watched you dance with Dave. You're very good."

"Thank you." She smiled at him and pushed her hair back. "I was watching you, too. You're very good yourself."

Jean said coolly, "Dance with me, Dave. Your friend is occupied."

Dave grinned and took the black-haired girl away.

"She hates me," Pat Cullum said wonderingly. "I hardly know her and she hates me."

Steve said lightly, "I imagine a lot of women do. And I don't suppose it bothers you much, does it?"

She laughed. "Not at all. What are you drinking?"

"Scotch and water. Why?"

"I always drink what the man I'm with drinks. It's a whim of mine."

"You're only with me momentarily," Steve pointed out. "You can get mighty sick mixing drinks, you know."

73

"I know," she said amiably. "But how do you know I'm only with you momentarily? You're not here with anyone else. I noticed."

He grinned at her. "Now, we don't want to annoy Dave. Not while he and I are working together."

She reached for her drink. "Don't you worry about Dave. He's dancing with his sad and secret love this second, and he's had enough whiskey to tell her about it."

Steve danced with her and they danced well, and the challenge of her body almost made him forget the significance of her perfume.

The crowd noise grew and the alcohol poured and someone fell into the pool. A fight started but was quickly broken up. A little after one o'clock Dotty asked Steve if he would help to encourage the guests to eat.

"Harry's disappeared somewhere," she explained. "We've just got to get some food and coffee into these drunks."

By two o'clock they had managed to inveigle some coffee into the drunker of the drunken and food into all the others. Steve's own fine edge had worn off by this time. He sat quietly with the script girl near the pool, nursing a big mug of coffee and scanning the crowd for Pat Cullum.

She was not in sight. Nor was Dave Sidney. Harry and a number of other men had come from the garage crap game. Practically all the people Steve knew were visible except for Dave and Pat. Perhaps it was just as well. Adultery had never been one of his comfortable vices.

He said good night to the Bergdahls and Dotty thanked him for helping to subdue the revelers, explaining loudly enough for most of the guests to hear that "Harry is *never* any good at parties."

74

He went around to the parking area, and it looked as though there was someone in his car.

There was. Pat Cullum looked up, rubbed her eyes, yawned and said, "It's about time!"

"Where's Dave?" Steve asked.

"He passed out. He's sleeping here tonight."

Steve got behind the wheel. "And with a yardful of handsome young men to choose from, you picked me. Why?"

"Call it a simple case of lust," she said. "Let's go."

NINE

She was active and demanding. She was artful and violent; her teeth brought blood from the lobe of his ear. Finally she was quiescent.

Her apartment was on the second floor of a fairly new building on a slope north of Hollywood. She had quite a view from her southern windows. It was not a cheap apartment.

On the broad, low bed, Steve stretched, spent and faintly uncomfortable. She was a girl who might soon demand more, and he was sure he could not supply the demand.

He said, "That's an unusual perfume you use."

"It ought to be, at fifty dollars a dram."

"Fifty dollars a dram . . . ! That's four hundred dollars an ounce."

"I guess. A man named Dostel makes it. He claims that each fragrance is tailored for only one person. But I'll bet he sells the same odor to women in other towns. This particular number is Dostel Number 263 if you're thinking of buying me some."

"At four hundred dollars an ounce? I'd have to give up smoking. Tell me, do you buy it for yourself?"

Her laugh was low and mocking. She asked, "Do you like peanut butter sandwiches?"

"I don't think so. Why?"

"I want one," she answered. "And a big glass of milk. Shall I bring you a drink?"

"No. But maybe the milk . . . Wait, I'll go with you."

They went to the kitchen, naked as sparrows, and she turned on the bright overhead light and pointed to a chair in the breakfast area. "You sit, I'll serve."

In her full, bronzed body there was no hint of sag. In her friendly, natural behavior there was no hint of shame.

She was reaching to open one of the cupboard doors when Steve said, "You were with Hart Jameson Wednesday night, weren't you? Why didn't you go to the police?"

She paused, her body tense, and turned to stare at him. "Are you crazy? I had a date Wednesday night. Why did you say that?"

"I smelled your perfume in his apartment when I went to see him. I know it was yours."

She continued to stare. "Is that why you came here, why you came up, to question me about Hart Jameson?"

Steve shook his head.

"You lie," she said hoarsely. "You've—spoiled *everything*."

He raised a hand. "Be sensible, listen to . . ."

"Listen, hell! Get out! Do you think I brought you here because you were a director or because you had money or because I was drunk? I wanted *you*, just as you are, just for tonight. Now, *get out!*"

Steve said quietly, "Please, will you listen to . . ."

She reached up and got a pitcher and she lifted it high. "I swear I'll kill you if you're not out of here in two minutes."

77

Her voice was loud enough to arouse the neighbors. It was that threat as much as the pitcher that sent Steve to the bedroom without further argument.

He dressed hurriedly. He was out in the cold night three minutes later.

There were only two cars in sight. One was his Bentley, in front of the apartment. The other, a green Pontiac half a block away on the other side of the street, was either Tomkevic's car or a duplicate.

Steve got into his car and started the engine. He drove almost to the Pontiac before switching on his headlights. And then he put them on the high beam.

Behind the windshield of the Pontiac the blank face of Tomkevic blinked in the sudden glare.

Had he followed Steve here or the girl? The car hadn't been there when they'd arrived. The detective had another item for his dossier. And a lever? A bit of blackmail he could use to pry some honest answers out of Steve?

No. He hadn't been up there very long. If he had stayed all night, Tomkevic would have had his lever.

It seemed to Steve the smell of perfume still lingered in the car. He drove slowly, watching to see if the green Pontiac would follow. There was a pressure in his chest again and a bad taste in his mouth.

Casual, he told himself, *think of it as that. A half-drunken romp in the hay with a girl who was begging for it. Casual . . .* Would he consider it casual if Marcia had been the guilty one?

The car swerved and the driver of the car flanking him sounded his horn angrily. Perspiration broke out on Steve's neck and forehead, and nausea expanded in his stomach.

That miserable, ubiquitous, tenacious Tomkevic. He might not be building a case solid enough to stand up in court, but he was probably building a case that would delay the payment of the insurance money to Harry.

Steve sucked deeply of the cold night air. He thought of Pat Cullum, naked in her bright kitchen, angrily eating a peanut butter sandwich, and he laughed to himself. But the nausea remained.

An incident, a casual nothing, a meaningless moment; how could any evil be read into that? He had been a tame domestic animal for a number of years. Tonight he had been a willing victim of circumstance. It had been a frustrating six months just past, and he had desperately needed the cathartic effect of this ridiculous night.

Adjusted now? he asked himself. A small lie, a trivial succumbing to blackmail, a momentary infidelity. Nothing to fret about, really. Nothing but the nausea.

He was in Beverly Hills, where the lots are wide and the houses set well back. He pulled to the curb and left the car and found some bushes and was sick.

He drove home carefully after that, alert for prowl cars and the green Pontiac. The clock on his instrument board showed exactly four o'clock when he left the car on the drive in front of the garage.

He slept without dreams and woke to a hot Sunday afternoon and a hangover. When he came into the living room, Mrs. Burke told him that Dave Sidney had phoned and left a number.

The number was Harry's and Steve dialed it.

Dave answered the phone. "I've been thinking of that bit with the torch singer, Steve. Don't you think Jean D'Arcy could handle that well?"

Steve smiled to himself. "Do you? Is this a form of non-family nepotism? Sweet on her, aren't you?"

"So, maybe. But you know I wouldn't risk spoiling the picture for anybody or anything. She's very good and she'll work at minimum."

79

"She can read for it," Steve said. "I've been thinking of that girl in the diving-board scene at the lake. And who would I be thinking of for that?"

"Pat Cullum. She's got the figure."

Steve asked, "But can she swim?"

"Swim?" Dave chuckled. "Like a mink." A pause. "I hope she got home all right last night."

"I'm sure she did. How are you and your drunken uncle feeling today?"

"Fit and happy. Look, why don't you come over for dinner, as long as Marcia is out of town?"

"I'd be bad company. At the moment I'm only looking for a hole to crawl into." He sighed. "We're taking care of our friends, aren't we?"

"The mark of a Harry Bergdahl picture," Dave said lightly. "Would it be all right if I came over later in the day? I'd like to talk with you."

"I guess. I should be human in a few hours. I'll be here."

He drank some tomato juice and ate some heavily buttered toast. He took the percolator of coffee and the Sunday papers out to the sundeck.

The death of Hart Jameson as news had retreated to one of the inner pages in the local news section. But as a feature story in the drama-arts section of the *Times*, it received the full lachrymose treatment.

There was a picture of Hart at the age of seven, riding a rented pony and staring belligerently into the camera. There were some stills from *Sunburst Alley* and a bleak shot of an Oklahoma orphanage where he had spent a few of the formative years.

There were quotes by personalities always ready with extravagant quotes. All in all, Hart Jameson had achieved an eminence in death he could very easily have missed by living.

Finally, on one of the inner pages where the text had

carried over, there was one more picture of Hart. He was standing with his arm around the jet-haired Jean D'Arcy. The caption asked: *Romance?*

The text informed the reader that the lovely television star, Jean D'Arcy, had been a frequent companion of Hart's in the East. It was rumored that she had followed him out here after a quarrel had sent him west.

Steve poured himself another cup of coffee. Maybe they wouldn't get Miss D'Arcy at minimum after today's publicity. Or maybe the inclusion of her name in the piece was the work of Harry's cunning hand?

No. Finding a spot for Jean had been Dave's idea, not Harry's. And it hadn't even been suggested until today.

The sun soaked him, baking out the alcohol. He ate two cold-beef sandwiches and drank some milk and spent an hour in the pool. He felt almost human when Dave Sidney arrived.

Dave didn't come alone. Jean D'Arcy was with him, and they had brought their swimming clothes.

"So it shouldn't be a total loss," Dave explained. "Jean wanted to read for that two-bit side, but I thought you might not be in a mood for that."

"I'm not," Steve answered. "Has Harry okayed it?"

Dave smiled. "He told me to tell you he has complete faith in your casting judgment."

"That was generous of him," Steve said dryly. He looked at Dave steadily. "Yesterday, you told him Marcia was out of town. How did you know that?"

Dave frowned. "Laura told me when I phoned her to see if she had a ride to the party. Why did you ask that, Steve?"

Steve shrugged.

Dave colored. "I guess we—caught you in a bad mood, didn't we?"

Steve sighed. "You did, and I apologize." He put a hand on Dave's shoulder. "Come on, let's get into that pool."

Jean D'Arcy's swim suit was an unrelieved white, trim and scanty. And though she lacked the extraordinary mammary and posterior development of Pat Cullum, Jean wore the suit to advantage.

Steve sat with a cigarette on the sunny side of the pool and watched Dave and the girl dive and swim. They were a well-matched couple, intelligent, personable and young. And innocent? The girl had been a companion of Hart Jameson's, and Dave was a much more complicated person than Steve had first assumed.

Jean came out of the water near where Steve sat and asked, "Would you light me a cigarette? My hands are wet."

Steve lighted her one and handed her a towel before giving her the cigarette. He said casually, "I see you had some publicity in today's *Times*."

She nodded. "Though it was all hogwash about my romance with Hart Jameson." She puffed deeply and looked candidly at Steve. "What happened to your ear?"

He reached a hand up in sudden remembrance. "I must have scraped it, diving. Is it bleeding?"

"The lobe is discolored. It looks as though somebody bit it."

Steve stared at her unblinkingly, and she met his gaze. Finally, he said with a smile, "I guess you heard Dave tell me Harry had complete faith in my casting judgment?"

She smiled in return. "I heard. Believe me, I had no idea my remark had any significance."

"It didn't," he said. "Was that story about you and Jameson in the paper a *complete* lie?"

"Almost. I didn't follow him out here; that's absurd. I did go to a few places with him in New York, but that

82

was because we were both studying at the Studio. We rarely went anywhere alone and we always went Dutch."

"Did you meet Mitchell Morton through him?"

"No. Mitch was at the Studio, too. I met him there." She smiled doubtfully. "Am I being interviewed or investigated?"

"Only making conversation," Steve answered. "One more question while Dave's out of earshot—do you like him?"

She made a face. "I like him, Uncle Steve. Do you like him?"

Steve nodded, and said with false gravity, "I was thinking of Pat Cullum for that bit you want to read for."

"It's your picture," she said, "yours to ruin with bad minor casting." She put her cigarette out in an ash tray, turned abruptly and dived into the pool.

The young ones, he thought, *the good young ones.* They were coming out here in swarms from New York, and what was there for them to do? Eastern television, which had started with such invigorating promise for the early hour-long dramas, was retrogressing to the 1912 cinema level. There was always a place for the bad actors, but what could the good ones do?

Dave came out of the water and padded over to pick up a towel. As he wiped the back of his neck, he asked, "Isn't she nice? Jean, I mean?"

"Very nice. What do you know about Mitchell Morton, Dave?"

Dave shrugged. "He's a good actor. He's hungry. But he's young enough so that doesn't matter."

"He's ambitious, too, isn't he? He'd go to some extremes, I would bet, to get his face in front of the public."

Dave frowned. "I guess. Steve, how far would you go to protect a picture you thought a lot of?"

Steve smiled and didn't answer.

Dave asked, "How about that—bit?"

"She can have it."

Dave sat down. "Thanks. What happened to your ear?"

"The housekeeper bit it last night," Steve explained carefully, "repelling my advances."

For seconds, they said nothing as they watched Jean swim the length of the pool and back. *The young ones,* Steve thought again, *the good young ones, the firm young ones, the ear-biters and the blackmailers.* At thirty-seven, he decided, the firm young ones looked so damned interesting. . . .

At seven it turned too cool to swim, and they went into the house to raid the refrigerator. After that they sat in the playroom, watching the image on the monster, this particular image being an hour-long comedy from New York.

The pair made caustic comments from time to time, but Steve rested, too well aware of the medium's limits to expect the perfection only the young demanded.

At ten-thirty Dave and Jean left, and the house seemed lonely. Steve went out to the front yard. It was a clear, cold night, and he could see the lights flashing along Sunset Boulevard.

It was then he remembered he had promised Marcia they would go up together today. She had gone to the camp alone, but he wondered if she had expected him to drive up to join her.

A car turned up from the highway below, and from a driveway a quarter of the way up the hill another car turned down, its headlights illuminating the car coming up.

84

It was the Buick, it was Marcia. He went over to the driveway to wait for her.

She had no greeting for him. Her face was grim, she avoided his eyes. He followed her from the garage to the kitchen, and she refused to look at him or answer his questions.

She was opening the refrigerator door when he went into his study. He sat there, smoking and staring at nothing, his thoughts black, his temper boiling. Who in hell did she think she was?

He heard her walking around in the kitchen and later he heard water running in the bathroom. But it was the guest bathroom. He heard a door close and there was silence.

In a few minutes he rose and went to their bedroom. She was not there. A nightgown and robe and pair of slippers were missing from her closet.

He went to the guest room. The door was closed. He opened it and turned on the bright overhead light. She was lying with her back to the doorway.

He said, "Marcia, I've a right to know why you're acting like this."

"You promised to come up," she said. "And I told the kids you had promised. And they waited for you. They waited and waited and waited."

"I'm very sorry about that. I went to a party at Bergdahl's last night and I didn't get home until late. I didn't wake up until this afternoon."

"Explain that to the children. Write them a letter and explain that, if you think you can."

He took a deep breath. "And how long do you intend to sleep in here?"

"Forever, probably."

With fine, unconscious hypocrisy, he said, "It's been over two weeks, you might remember. And I'm not made of stone."

She said quietly and coldly, "It's been over two weeks for me. I'm not sure it has for you."

His stomach churned and his hands trembled. He looked at her back doubtfully. "God damn it," he said, "turn around!"

She turned over to glare at him.

He asked, "Just exactly what did you mean by that last crack?"

Her voice was even and calm and cold. "You've been going downhill morally so fast lately it wouldn't surprise me to learn you had tried *anything*. And one of Harry Bergdahl's parties would be a logical place to start off on an adultery kick."

"You don't mean that."

"I mean that."

He said hoarsely, "I'm thinking of the kids. That's all that's keeping me home tonight."

She turned over again. She said wearily, "Turn out the light and get out of here. Don't threaten me—not until you're ready to do it in court."

The fever of unrighteous indignation burned in him, and he said harshly, "I'll be glad to go into court any time you're ready."

"I'm ready now," she said. "Good night."

He stared at her familiar back, and the sickness welled in him again and his knees trembled. A life without Marcia would be worse than death. A life without Marcia and the kids would be . . .

He couldn't imagine it. He said softly, "I hope you'll be more reasonable tomorrow." He turned out the light and closed the door gently.

TEN

He sat for an hour in his unlighted study, thinking back on it all from Laura's first bit of gossip. That had been Wednesday, as they drove home from Santa Barbara.

And after he had gone to see Jameson that same evening, a few new facts had been revealed to him. He could see no pattern in them but if he gave them to Tomkevic, perhaps the detective could.

What then was preventing him from phoning Tomkevic? The unadmitted fear that Bergdahl was the murderer? If Harry wasn't, the insurance money was safe. If Harry was, did he want him revealed?

Harry's own nephew wanted to *know;* he wasn't afraid of the truth. But Harry's own nephew wasn't thirty-seven years old and he wasn't carrying the financial load Steve was. He could afford his militant morality.

He thought back on John Abbot's phrase: "the sanctity of solvency." John could afford morality, too. He had been active in a seller's market before the days of confiscatory taxation.

Your job is making pictures, Steven Leander, not moral judgments. That would be the pragmatic view. If he had sinned, they had been sins of omission. Overlooking, of course, one small sin of commission on Pat Cullum's wide, low bed.

87

Tomkevic was not concerned with sin; he was concerned with crime. Though the crime that concerned him now was also a sin, the sin of murder.

I am innocent of murder. So far as I know there has been no murder.

That was the thought that he took to bed with him—so far as he knew, there had been no murder. It helped to bolster the righteousness of his anger over the deportment of his unreasonable wife.

It didn't help him to sleep. But there were pills for that, and he took them after the first restless hour, falling asleep to dream of his personal Javert, the brush-haired, brown-eyed, soft-voiced Tomkevic.

Marcia didn't join him at breakfast. Mrs. Burke served him with a minimum of dialogue, and Steve wondered if she had overheard last night's quarrel. He had finished eating by the time Dave came, and they left immediately to pick up Laura.

Steve had always managed to divorce his personal troubles from his professional problems. Today he didn't achieve this. He was short-tempered and sarcastic. He had a hopelessly disrupted cast halfway through the morning's shooting.

He knew he was dealing with temperamental people and he knew he was handling them badly. But some perversity in him persisted. His temper grew shorter and his tongue sharper.

They stopped for a break at ten-thirty, and Laura came over to tell him quietly, "You'll have a mutiny on your hands any minute. What's wrong, Steve?"

"Everything," he said curtly. "You know you're not delivering, don't you?"

She flushed. "No, I didn't. But I'll take your word for it." Her voice was bitter. "Possibly the role is too big for me."

He almost said *possibly* but stopped in time. He said, "It seems to be too much for you this morning. It wasn't Friday."

She started to say something, paused, and turned away. He watched her walk over to the table where Dave sat and take a seat next to him. Dave glanced guiltily at Steve before he and Laura started to talk.

Tom Leslie came over to ask genially, "Am I really that lousy, Steve, or are you having a bad morning?"

Steve said evenly, "You weren't lousy. You were just barely—adequate, to use the critics' cliché. I expect something better than that."

Leslie continued to smile. "I think we're all trying to give you something better than that." He paused. "We—could stand a little patience."

Steve stared at him for seconds. "Mr. Leslie, you haven't been in this business very long, but I'm sure you've been in it long enough to learn the director is *never* argued with."

Leslie's smile turned cold. "I've learned that, Mr. Leander. I'll remember it from now on."

Steve watched him walk over to join Laura and Dave at the table. And he knew this would be a lost day. And he knew it was his fault. Or Marcia's? Or Bergdahl's? Or Tomkevic's?

Laura rode home with Tom Leslie. Dave came back with Steve. Dave was unusually quiet.

After about twenty minutes of silent driving, Steve said, "Okay, speak up. Who's leading the mutiny?"

Dave smiled weakly. "Boy, you were edgy today. Were they that bad?"

"Probably not. But they were so great Friday, and I suppose my own—state of mind magnified the letdown."

"Are you still thinking about Hart Jameson?"

Steve nodded without taking his eyes from the road. "Aren't you?"

"Mmmm-hmmm. But it looks more like an accident every day."

"Did you learn anything, Dave, that the police don't know?"

Dave paused before saying too casually, "Nothing important."

"Anything I should know?"

"Nothing," Dave said definitely. "Can't we talk about something else?"

"All right. Let's talk about the picture. Are we going to be able to finish it?"

"I don't know. I don't see why not. Uncle Harry is very good at raising money and he has over half of it."

There was a long and uncomfortable silence. Finally Dave said, "Ever since Jameson's death you've been—different. It's none of my business, but is it because of the quarrel with Marcia?"

"Partly, I suppose," Steve admitted. "Though I was never an easy man to get along with while working. I —expect too much from people."

"And too much from yourself, maybe? And at the moment, you might be hating yourself?"

Steve said slowly, "That could be. Since I lied to the police about why I went to see Jameson, I've been— unhappy."

"That's easily corrected, Steve. Go to them and tell them you lied. Tell them the real reason you went to see Jameson."

"That would involve your uncle. Do you want me to do that?"

"No."

"So . . . ?"

Dave said earnestly, "*I* wouldn't want my uncle involved, but do you always do what others want you to do? I'd rather see Uncle Harry involved than see you do a bad job on the picture."

90

Steve said gently, "Don't worry, I'll come to terms with myself. We had a good day Friday, and there'll be more of them."

There had been, he reflected, a funeral and a party since Friday, and both had added to his general despondency. There might be more revelations in store, though he hadn't actively sought any.

Would it help, he wondered, if he could prove to himself that Harry wasn't a murderer? And how could he prove it to himself? Perhaps by coöperating with Tomkevic or the police, by telling them all he knew that they didn't.

Though they had a gardener three times a week, Marcia was out in front feeding the roses when Steve drove up. Marcia liked to work when she was emotionally disturbed.

She smiled at Dave and ignored Steve. She didn't speak to either of them.

Dave said quietly, "I'll see you tomorrow." He went directly to his car.

Steve started to walk over toward Marcia and then decided against it. He went into the house through the garage.

In his study he looked up Dostel in the western phone book. There were four in his end of town, and one of them was Dostel Laboratories, Inc. This had the same address as a Paul Dostel. He dialed the residence number.

A pleasant voice answered, "Dostel Laboratories, Paul Dostel speaking," and Steve asked, "Are you the Dostel who makes those individualized perfumes?"

"Yes."

"My name is Leander. Would it be possible for me to see you this evening?"

"Steven Leander, the director?"

"That's right."

"I'll be here all evening, Mr. Leander."

Steve thanked him and hung up. If he should learn that Jameson had bought the perfume Pat Cullum used, it would seem to indicate she had been the girl in Hart's apartment.

And if she was? What did he do with the knowledge? Take it to the police? Or Tomkevic?

He could decide that when he learned more. He didn't mix a drink this evening. He went directly in for his shower.

Dinner was quiet. Marcia spoke when spoken to, maintaining a rigid formality. He stopped speaking to her after the first few minutes.

He was on his coffee when Bergdahl phoned.

"A little birdie told me something," Harry said coyly. "He told me you had trouble today on the set."

"A little birdie named Dave?" Steve asked.

"Not him. I'm his dumb uncle, remember? To be frank, Tom Leslie phoned me."

"I had to put him in his place, that's true," Steve said.

"His place . . . ?" A pause. "What's his place?"

"Subordinate to the director. I'm sure we all agree on that. At least he did."

A sigh. "Well, when I see the rushes, I'll know if the day was wasted." Another pause. "Is something bothering you, Steve?"

"A number of things, all personal. Don't worry about me, Harry. I'm coming out of it."

"Good. You got any problems you need help on, old Harry's here every minute, right?"

"Right. Thanks for calling."

He hung up, annoyed. Leslie had gone over his head. He had figured the man for more of a trouper than that.

When he went back to the table to finish his coffee, Marcia looked at him inquiringly but said nothing.

"Bergdahl," Steve said. "I was owly today and Tom Leslie complained to him about it."

Marcia nodded, saying nothing.

Steve sat down and looked at her. "We're not children. This is unnatural behavior for us. Shall I tell you why I went to see Hart Jameson that night?"

"It's not important any more," she answered.

"Not important . . . ? Why not? If you love me, it's important."

"I used to love you and admire you," she said. "I think I need to do both—or neither."

He kept his temper from his voice. "That's—soap opera. You're too intelligent to talk that way."

"It's the way I feel, Steve."

"All right. I'm sorry about Sunday. If you had stayed home Friday, we both would have gone up to camp Sunday. That was the way we planned it."

She said nothing.

"I haven't the best disposition in the world," he went on, "but you've known that for a long time. Why is this last flare-up any more important than the others?"

"I've learned to live with your disposition," she said, "and your childish insecurity. Because you were honest and dedicated, I could take a lot of nonsense. I can't live with dishonesty."

"That's what I'm trying to correct now, a temporary dishonesty. And you told me it wasn't important any more."

"Let's talk about it later," she said wearily.

"I'd like to talk about it now. You're failing me, Marcia. I need your moral support *now*."

Her smile was cynical. "*I'm* failing *you*? Even if it were true, it would be the first time, wouldn't it?"

Anger grew in him but he maintained a calm voice. "No. You have the impossible code of a person who *never* had to worry about money. I think it's fair to say you have never tried to understand the problems of people who weren't that lucky."

"I understand your problems," she argued. "It's your behavior that I can't understand. I don't want to talk about it, Steve."

Harsh words came to his tongue but he held them back. "All right, Judge," he said smilingly. "Yes, Your Honor." He stood up. "I have to see a man this evening. I won't be late."

She nodded and said nothing.

Damn her, damn her, damn her . . . And all her smug and gilt-edged friends. There wasn't a damned one of them who had the faintest idea of what was going on in the working world.

As he drove over to the address of Paul Dostel, Steve wondered why he had suddenly decided to inquire into the death of Hart Jameson. And the guilty thought came that perhaps it was because of today's wasted film. The death of Hart Jameson had finally begun to interfere with the successful creation of a motion picture. *His* picture.

Well, there were a number of reasons for morality, not all of them admirable.

Paul Dostel looked like a skinny Yul Brynner, a tall, thin, bright-eyed man with a head as hairless as a cue ball.

His apartment was above and behind the one-story brick laboratory that fronted on the street. It was an elegant apartment, and Mr. Dostel wore a rather ornate lounging robe and alligator slippers.

After Steve was seated in the living room, Dostel said, "I imagine you're here to see about a fragrance, and I can hope it's for your wife." He sighed. "So few of my clients order for their wives."

"Most of your clients are men?"

"About two-thirds. You're married to Marcia Bishop, aren't you, Mr. Leander?"

Steve nodded. "Did you look that up after I phoned?"

Dostel shook his head. "I keep myself informed as well as possible about the histories of our more socially prominent women. Sometimes, you see, an odor that brings back a pleasant memory is all my client is seeking. This is a complicated business, dealing in intangibles, and the more I know about my clients' backgrounds, the more success I'm likely to have."

Steve smiled politely. "It sounds like a fascinating business. However, I'm not here to buy. I'm here for information."

"Oh . . . ?"

The single exclamation had been meant to show surprise. Paul Dostel had voiced it badly, and there had been no surprise on his face.

"Yes," Steve said. "I'd like to know who your customer, or client, is for Number 176."

Now there was surprise on the face of Paul Dostel. He asked doubtfully, "One seventy-six . . . ?" before he recovered his composure.

Steve smiled. "Did I say 176? I meant 263."

A silence while Dostel stared at him. Finally he said, "I never reveal the names of my clients. I think you can understand why. I explained it a few moments ago."

"I'm not looking for scandal," Steve said. "I'm looking for information that might uncover a murderer."

Dostel frowned. "A murderer . . . ? Who has been murdered, Mr. Leander?"

"It's possible Hart Jameson was murdered."

"And one of my perfumes is involved, somehow?"

Steve nodded.

Dostel continued to frown. "Then why haven't the police contacted me? You're not working for the police, are you?"

"Not officially," Steve said. He stood up. "Well, I suppose you're right. This is their business, not mine. I'll tell them about the perfume." He half turned toward the door.

"One moment, Mr. Leander," Dostel said thoughtfully.

Steve waited.

Dostel said slowly, "I can't afford to court any unpleasant publicity. Would you mind telling me where you learned about my fragrance 263?"

"I'd mind," Steve answered shortly. "I'm not looking for scandal and I certainly don't intend to spread it."

Dostel took a deep breath. "You realize, I hope, that you are forcing me to violate an important professional principle for the first time?"

"I'll take your word for it."

Dostel rose. "The information is downstairs in the office. I'll be right back."

Steve was almost sure the other man would come back with a fraudulent name. But if he did, that, too, would be a straw.

He came back with a small file card in his hand. He read aloud: "Edward Ambrose Brown, 730 South Plumer Street, Tucson, Arizona." He looked at Steve blandly. "Is that any help, Mr. Leander?"

Steve shook his head. "It has no meaning for me. But perhaps it will have for the police. Isn't there some other local customer that fragrance could have been sold to?"

Dostel shook his head. "One client to a fragrance, that's my guarantee. Of course, I have no way of knowing who Mr. Brown bought the perfume for."

"I thought you said you like to know the backgrounds of the people who use your perfume?"

"I did say that. And I do like to. But it's not always possible."

"I see. What is the price of that Number 263?"

"Fifty dollars a dram, four hundred dollars an ounce."

Steve thanked him and left. He was only about two blocks from the Hotel Beauchamp. He walked over.

And there, in a Tucson telephone book, he looked up Edward Ambrose Brown and found a man by the name of Edward A. Brown at 730 South Plumer. If Dostel was lying, it had been a careful lie.

He went back to his car and drove north. On a slope north of Hollywood, he parked in front of a fairly new apartment building and stared at the light in a second-floor window.

He had left there hurriedly Sunday morning, and he wondered if Miss Pat Cullum was inclined to nurse a grudge. It seemed reasonable to guess she wouldn't relish his coming back with questions.

Well, he had gone this far . . . He got out of the car and went up to the second floor to ring her bell.

She was wearing a white knit dress tonight and her hair was up. She stared at him and said, "Migawd, you're not gutless, are you?"

He smiled. "I came with an apology, an offer and a question. Should I leave?"

She studied him. "Come in."

"If you'll promise not to throw any crockery."

"I promise. You can forget the apology. What kind of offer did you have in mind?" She held the door wide.

Steve came in. "A nothing, really. A very small bit in this picture we're making. It involves wearing a swimming suit and posing on a diving board. A few lines might be written in."

"I'll take it," she said. "Now, what was the question?"

"Do you know a man named Edward Ambrose Brown?"

She looked at him blankly. "So help me, I've never even heard the name. Am I supposed to know him?"

"Mr. Dostel told me half an hour ago that Edward Ambrose Brown is the only purchaser of Number 263."

"You can tell Mr. Dostel from me that he's a god-damned liar. And if you want to know where I was Wednesday night from nine o'clock until way past midnight, I can give you the names of three people who were with me."

"You don't need to do that," Steve said. "I'm not a detective."

"Even if you were," she said, "you wouldn't learn from me who gave me the perfume. But I can guarantee you it didn't come from Jameson."

"I didn't assume it did," Steve told her. "Well, perhaps the person who gave you the perfume is a friend of this Brown. That can be checked, I suppose."

She shrugged.

Steve said, "I don't want to crowd you, but do you think you're acting in your own best interest? There's a possibility Mr. Jameson was murdered. I'm sure you're not equipped to protect yourself against a murderer, Pat."

"Possibly not," she agreed. "But if I wanted protection, wouldn't the Police Department be the logical place to go for it?"

He nodded.

She smiled. "You wouldn't want me to go there, would you?"

"Why not?"

"I don't know why not. But knowing what you do about the perfume, why didn't you go to the police?"

He looked at her candidly. "Because I think you're innocent of murder or involvement in murder. And, thinking that, I certainly wouldn't want to involve you in an embarrassing investigation."

"I've been told that any kind of publicity is good publicity."

"Not today. However, I'm not your father, am I? And you're of age."

Her smile was mocking. "I'm of age. And I hope you're not my father. You know, Steve, I think you might be a nice guy if you could ever forget how important you are."

"Thank you," he said coolly. "I'll have somebody get in touch with you about that bit. Good night, Miss Cullum."

"Good night, Steve," she said lightly. "Drop in any time."

ELEVEN

A faint resentment flickered in him as he went down the steps to the street and over to his car. He climbed in behind the wheel and looked at the lighted street ahead. *Where next, Dick Tracy?*

A green Pontiac came up from behind and parked in front of his car. Steve waited.

Tomkevic got out on the street side and walked behind his car, heading for the apartment building.

Steve leaned over and called, "Mr. Tomkevic!"

The investigator turned, frowned and then walked toward the Bentley as Steve opened the door.

He stood there without getting in. "I'm not here to see you."

"I didn't think you were. Would you sit in the car for a few minutes?"

Tomkevic looked up at the lighted window and then stepped into the car. "Decided to turn honest, Leander?"

"A little. What interest do you have in Miss Cullum?"

"Frankly, only a suspicion because of your interest in her. You're still my key to this puzzle."

"This much I'll tell you about her," Steve said. "She wears the same perfume as the girl who was in Jameson's apartment the night he died. And the man who makes the perfume told me an hour ago each individual fragrance is sold to only one customer."

"Oh . . . ? What's the man's name?"

Steve told him and gave him a full account of his conversation with Dostel. And he told him about the Brown he'd found at the right address in the Tucson phone book.

Tomkevic took out a card and handed it to Steve. Then he wrote Brown's name and address in a notebook. "I can check that easily enough. He could be a friend of this Dostel, you know."

"I suppose it's more than possible. You're not going to tell Miss Cullum I gave you this information, are you?"

"No. I'll tell her I'm checking her because she was a friend of Hart Jameson's."

"Was she?"

"Yes. And young Sidney brought her to the party, didn't he? And he's a nephew of Harry Bergdahl's. Now, what excuse could I have for giving up on this case?"

Steve didn't answer.

Tomkevic asked, "Is that why you came home with the Cullum girl Saturday night, because you were trying to learn something?"

"Partly."

Tomkevic looked out at the street. Finally, "I was going to be a real son-of-a-bitch, Leander. I was going to tell your wife you brought that bomb up there home Saturday night."

"Why . . . ?"

"To stir up some action. Quite often truth comes out of turbulence."

"What made you think I hadn't told my wife I brought this—bomb home Saturday night?"

Tomkevic said dryly, "I'm a married man. I know I wouldn't have told *my* wife, not if she'd ever seen the girl."

"My wife has never seen Miss Cullum."

There was a silence, which Steve broke. "I've given you some help. Now give me this—if Jameson was murdered, who is your favorite suspect?"

"Until five minutes ago," Tomkevic said candidly, "you were."

"*I* was . . . ? I was at a movie with my wife. You knew that."

"How could I be sure? I have a long list of wives who lied to protect their husbands. And that's why I was going to—create this domestic turbulence."

There was another silence, and this time Tomkevic broke it. "Why are you getting interested in Jameson's death?"

"I'm trying to resolve a moral dilemma I found myself in."

"I figured you would, eventually. And there's a possibility you could learn things I couldn't. You already have. Do you want to work with me? I mean unofficially, informally, of course."

"And possibly cost poor Harry Bergdahl a quarter of a million dollars? And put myself out of work? Do you realize what you're asking?"

"I do. And you were well aware of all those potentials when you decided to investigate for yourself."

Steve pointed out, "I was looking for innocence. You're asking me to help you establish guilt."

"I don't think you were looking for innocence. I think you were merely looking for information. To forestall a decision on your moral dilemma. But the decision would have to be made eventually if you learned what you didn't want to learn. Am I right?"

"I don't know. It all sounds very logical, but I can't seem to establish my motives as clearly as that."

Tomkevic smiled. "I'm heartened to find a man wrestling with a moral problem. It isn't a situation I've come upon recently."

Steve said lightly, "I'll give you a moral problem of your very own to ponder—you could be stopping production on a worth-while motion picture. And when was the last time you saw one of *those?*"

Tomkevic chuckled. "That's not a moral problem. That's an aesthetic problem. And what would a dumb Polack like me know about aesthetics? Carry on, Leander, keep in touch. I've got to run up and see that bomb before her date gets here."

"Who's her date? Someone I know?"

"A man named Mitchell Morton," Tomkevic answered. "Small damned world, isn't it?"

Small, damned, tight world. Revolving around a sun named Harry Bergdahl. Steve started the engine and turned back toward Sunset. He drove over to Laura's.

In her flush days Laura had owned one of the most impressive estates in Beverly Hills. The apartment she lived in now was not cheap, but it was a number of plateaus below her former eminence.

She opened her door and said with surprise, "This is an unexpected pleasure."

Clichés for all occasions, Steve thought, and smiled. "I was going by, so I thought I'd stop in to apologize."

"Going by alone or is Marcia in the car?"

"Alone," Steve answered. "I was a beast today, wasn't I?"

"Come in," she said.

He came into a small living room crowded with massive furniture, undoubtedly remnants from her former home.

103

"Drink?" she asked.

He sat down on a carved walnut davenport upholstered in mohair. "No, thanks. Tom Leslie complained to Harry about my treatment of him."

Laura sighed and looked at the floor. "Tom's—young and temperamental."

Steve nodded. "And not completely trustworthy, I'm beginning to suspect. Are you going to Santa Barbara with him tomorrow, or shall I pick you up as usual?"

She stared at him blankly. "Tomorrow . . . ? I was notified that we weren't working tomorrow."

"When?"

"About an hour ago. Are we working?"

"Not if you were notified. Harry must have had a brainstorm. He's probably been trying to get me. May I use your phone?"

She inclined her head toward the dinette. "It's in there."

Harry answered the phone and Steve asked, "What's this I hear about not working tomorrow?"

"That's right. I've been trying to call you. I've had a chance to look over the film, and we don't need any more from up there. We can fake the rest."

"No, Harry."

"What's *that?*"

"We can't fake the rest. We can't fake anything. I've got this picture firmly in mind now, and we have to go up there for at least two more days."

"Oh . . . ? You got the picture in mind? You got the money, too?"

"No. Haven't you?"

A silence. Then, "Look, Steve, don't go off half cocked. Don't say anything you'll be sorry for later."

"I'm trying not to. May I come over and see you now?"

"Not tonight, Steve. I've got an important engagement in twenty minutes and I'm leaving right now. We can talk it over tomorrow."

"When tomorrow? Could we make the date now?"

"Stevie, Stevie boy, what kind of talk is this—make the date? Do we have to be formal? Tomorrow. I'll call you or you call me, whoever gets up first."

"All right, Harry. I'll see you tomorrow."

"Sure. And cool off, huh? Today's been a bad one for you."

Steve hung up and went back to the living room. "Cut-rate Harry is back in form," he said bitterly. "We are about to create a turkey."

Laura said soothingly, "Easy now, Steve. Harry's the man who understands money. That's the first concern in any business, you know, to show a profit."

"I'll match the profits on my five best pictures against the total of any *fifteen* of his. The intelligent way to make money is to make a good picture."

"Always, Steve?"

"It's the safest. It's the surest. Unless you're making Grade-Z quickies. Christ, why did I ever get tied up with that man?"

Laura said nothing, staring at the floor.

Steve said wearily, "Well, I'm going home. Relax tomorrow. If I have to, I'll settle for one more day in Santa Barbara. But if that happens, it will be a long day and you'll need all the energy you can store up."

She rose. "All right, Steve. And watch your temper."

He came over to kiss her forehead. "I'll try. Lady, you were sensational Friday. And you will be again."

He drove home. He sat for some minutes in the car after killing the engine. He thought of the three people he had visited tonight and of Tomkevic. But mostly he thought of Laura, who had come from the estate in Beverly Hills to that apartment.

Tomorrow he would be going up against Harry Bergdahl for the first time since they were allied. He would be fighting for what he considered a major decision and Harry undoubtedly considered minor. His position would seem unreasonable to Harry, the capricious arrogance of a pretentious man.

He went into the house and found Marcia reading in the living room. She looked up to say, "John Abbot phoned. He wants you to call him." She went back to her reading.

"Thank you," Steve said formally. He went into the study to phone.

Abbot said, "I hear there's a possibility of money trouble on your picture."

"It's possible, John. Harry doesn't confide in me too much about the financial end, but you're probably right. Where did you hear the rumor?"

Abbot chuckled. "From one of my stoolies."

"Marcia, maybe?"

"No. What made you ask that, Steve?"

"I don't know. We're having money troubles, John."

"Well, that's why I phoned. I've a few contacts left, you know, and I've been scouting around. I'm positive I can get you some money if the picture looks promising."

"Thanks, John. Of course, the money is really Harry's department."

"But if you had a source, it would be a weapon, wouldn't it?" A pause. "You could afford to stay honest."

"You *have* been talking to Marcia."

"This wasn't her idea."

"I see. Well, thank you very much. Even if we don't need it, the knowledge that it's available is a—weapon. How are you feeling, John?"

"Like an old man. But that's in character. Steve, I've heard some surprising rumors about you around town."

"Did you believe them?"

"Not completely. Are you all right?"

"Is anybody ever? I'm struggling. I'm not in the ministry, John."

Abbot chuckled again. "No, you certainly are not. You call me, now, if it's necessary, Steve."

"I'll call you even if it isn't," Steve answered. "As soon as this picture is finished, we'll go fishing again, like we used to."

"Sure."

"And thank you again," Steve said. "Thank you very much."

He went back to the living room. Marcia continued to read. He said, "Harry's starting to give me trouble."

She didn't lift her eyes from the book. "Is that supposed to be news?"

"I thought it might be of interest to you," he said stiffly. He went into the study and turned on the television set.

Garbage, garbage, garbage . . . This was the machine that had crippled his industry. And only because his own industry had built up a public hunger for garbage.

That was what Harry Bergdahl understood, garbage. God damn it, Harry didn't need him for that. But he had thought he needed him or he never would have hired him. Had something changed his mind?

He went to bed early but couldn't fall asleep. He thought about tomorrow and wondered about tonight, wondered if he would hear Marcia's step in the hall, hear her come into the room.

He lay quietly and anxiously, waiting for a reconciliation. He didn't fall asleep until long after he heard her go into the guest room.

TWELVE

Dotty said, "Come in, Steve. Harry's taking a shower. He'll be out in a few minutes."

Steve came into the low-beamed, provincial living room and sat on a davenport near the high-hearth fireplace.

"Drink?" Dotty asked.

"Never in the morning," he answered. He smiled at her. "Recovered from the party, have you?"

Her answering smile was vacant and superficial. She looked at him anxiously. "Are you and Harry fighting about something?"

"Not yet," Steve said mildly.

"Money," she said. "It's money, I'll bet. It's all he fights about. He's been a horrible bear, lately." She looked at Steve closely. "It is only money, isn't it? He's been so nasty and secretive."

"Is the honeymoon over, Dotty?"

"Honeymoon . . . ? In a motel, that's where we spent our honeymoon. He never wanted to get out of bed except to go to the bathroom. Why don't you answer my questions, Steve? Why are you covering up?"

Steve said firmly, "I'm not covering up anything. Harry thinks we've shot enough film in Santa Barbara, and I don't. So we're going to discuss it this morning."

"That isn't all. You had trouble with Tom Leslie, too. I heard about that. Tom's a troublemaker, Steve."

"All the young talents give us occasional trouble, Dotty. I'm not worried about Tom."

She leaned over to take a cigarette from a box on the coffee table. Under the loose V of her blouse, Steve could see her firm breasts. She was wearing no bra. He looked away as he fumbled for a match.

Again she leaned forward to get the light he held for her. He said softly, "Easy, sister, that's a loose blouse. And I'm not as old as you think."

"Old . . . ?" She blew smoke into his face. "You're a kid, compared to Harry. Does Pat Cullum think you're old?"

Steve looked at her blankly. "Who's Pat Cullum?"

"Huh!" she said. "Don't give me that innocent look. I've got ears."

"All right," he said, "then *you* tell *me* what's eating Harry."

She sat on the davenport near him. "I wish I knew. I wish to hell I knew." She stared at the fireplace. "Do you think it could be connected to Hart Jameson's death? And that insurance policy?"

"I suppose it could. But how?"

"That's what I don't want to think about," she said quietly. "And then that damned detective pestering him . . ."

Steve said gently, "Look, Dotty, we know Harry's no murderer. It's probably money that's bothering him."

"We don't know anything," she said. "We don't *really* know anything about anybody."

Steve glanced over quickly, startled by the despair in her voice. She looked lonely and frightened, staring at the high-hearth fireplace.

Then Harry was there in a toweling robe and straw

slippers, his hair wet, his face unshaven. "Cuddling on the couch, you two, huh? A guy can't even take a shower any more."

Dotty stood up without smiling. Steve's smile was purely facial. Dotty said, "Steve thinks he's too old for me."

Harry looked at her without expression. "Business, honey. Run along."

She went out without another word. Harry came over to take the seat she'd vacated. "Well, Steve, speak your piece."

"It's simple enough. I need two more days up there."

"I want to show you the film, how we can cut it and fake the rest. You'll wait until I show you that, won't you?"

Steve said nothing, thinking.

Harry said, "Jesus, Laura was lousy yesterday."

"They were all bad, Harry."

"Not Leslie. Wait until you see the film. Leslie was all right."

"It's his scene," Steve pointed out. "He has to be better than all right in it. Are we running short of money, Harry?"

"We could, if that damned Polack keeps stalling things. Anyway, what's wrong with saving money on a picture? That's a sin?"

"At times. I might be able to get some money if we can show the investors the potential of a first-class picture." He paused, to drop the name with emphasis. "John Abbot phoned me last night."

Harry was silent, respectfully silent. "Abbot, huh? He's a friend of yours, isn't he?"

"Yes."

Harry frowned. "Jesus, I don't know. He'd want a bigger hunk of it than he's entitled to. He's all business, that Abbot."

"I don't think it would be his money."

Harry stared. "So then what does he want? A big commission for introducing us to the money?"

"Of course not," Steve said patiently. "He simply wants to help me. He's a friend."

Harry's laugh was short. "I got dozens of friends. Some of 'em have money. That don't mean they want to give me some of it. Stevie boy, there's got to be an angle. John Abbot's no dummy."

Steve was silent, realizing the impossibility of explaining to Harry about friends.

Harry said, "Maybe he wants to be like a silent partner? Maybe it would be that you got a bigger hunk of the picture, and you two would be silent partners?"

Steve laughed. "Harry, for heaven's sake, you're calling me a crook!"

Harry shook his head. "Nothing like that. No, Steve, I don't want to tangle with John Abbot."

Steve's hands trembled. He sat quietly, not looking at Harry. Finally he said, "Ask any of them what they think about yesterday's film. Ask Dave."

"That snot-nose? Since when is a writer consulted? Why should I ask anybody? Am I a greenhorn, am I new to the business?"

Steve said slowly, "Maybe to this kind of picture you're new, Harry."

In the silence, Steve thought he could hear his heart pound.

After a few seconds, Bergdahl asked quietly, "Make that clearer. What kind of crack was that?"

Steve forced himself to look at Harry fully. "Don't you agree that this picture is more—serious than most of those you've produced? You were known for your series pictures, Harry."

"*Were* known? I'm still known. Would you like to take a look at their grosses?"

"Let's not quibble, Harry. I'm sure both of us can quote some impressive figures. One question though—why did you want me? I didn't come to you, remember."

"You're a director. I needed a director. You're a good director and you weren't working."

"And as a good director, I'm asking for two more days in Santa Barbara. I'm not asking for the moon, you know."

"As a director," Harry said implacably, "you're entitled to ask. As the producer, I got a right to decide whether I let you. That's right, isn't it?"

"Technically, yes. But we discussed the possibility of friction before I signed. And you promised me a free hand with this picture."

Harry started to answer but was interrupted by a voice behind them. The voice was Dave Sidney's and it was indignant. "That's right, Uncle Harry. And you promised me, too, that Steve would have a free hand."

Startled, Harry turned to face his nephew. "Where'd you come from? Who invited you into this?"

Dave said stubbornly, "You promised before I signed. It's my script you want to ruin. I'll take it to the Guild."

Harry looked at Steve and shook his head. "He'll take it to the Guild. He's threatening me." He looked again at Dave. "What will you take?"

"Your promise. I sold you the script with the agreement that Steve was not to be interfered with."

Harry smiled contemptuously. "I promised? In writing?"

"No," Dave said evenly, "not in writing. But before a witness." He looked over at Dotty, standing in the doorway to the dining room.

Harry glanced coldly between his nephew and his wife. "What is this? What's going on here?"

112

Dotty said, "That's right, Harry, you promised Dave. I was there when you promised."

Bergdahl's face was grim and ugly. "Get out of here, both of you. I'm discussing business. Go!"

"Come on, Dave," Dotty said softly.

But Dave stood rigidly, glaring at his uncle. "I warn you, Uncle Harry, I've got a case."

"One more word out of you," Bergdahl said harshly, "and you'll wind up driving a bakery truck. Go, right now!"

Dave turned and walked out toward the dining room. Harry turned around again, breathing heavily. "Crazy," he said. "They're both crazy. He must have been in the kitchen all the time."

Steve rose. "I guess we've nothing to discuss, Harry. I don't know what's happened to you."

"Sit down, God damn it!" Bergdahl said hoarsely. "You, too?"

Steve asked quietly, "Has something happened, Harry? Is there something I don't know about that's frightening you?"

Bergdahl glared at him. "Frightening *me?* What scares me? Nothing scares me." Saliva flecked his lips.

"You're a lucky man, then. A number of things scare me. At the moment, you're one of them."

"I scare you? That's good. I'm glad to hear it. Maybe you'll listen to some sense if you get scared enough."

"I think I'd better go," Steve said. "We can talk about this later."

Harry looked up coldly. "Maybe you got a better job, huh? Maybe that's why John Abbot called you?"

Steve shook his head. "I've no new job nor prospects, Harry. But maybe I'd better look for one."

Harry said balefully, "Sit down. We're not through talking. You came here to talk. Sit down."

Steve stood for a moment looking down at Harry doubtfully. Then he smiled and said, "Okay, boss." He sat down.

"You bastard," Harry said. "You know the right words, don't you? You're good with words."

"I made a living from words for four years, Harry. And while we're on the subject, I think you were unnecessarily rude to Dave. You might need him someday. Someday he's going to be very good with words."

"He'll learn respect for his superiors first, or he won't get the chance to be good."

Steve took a deep breath. He had come here to reason, hoping that logic would prevail. It hadn't. He said, "I think we both need a drink, don't you, Harry?"

Harry nodded. He sighed. His body was slumped in an attitude of resignation, but there was no surrender in his broad face. He mixed a pair of drinks, and Steve lifted his.

"To better understanding," Steve said.

"That I'll drink to." Bergdahl downed half of his at a gulp.

Steve said quietly, "One long day could do it up there, Harry. How about settling for one long day?"

"All right, all right! You think I'm chintzy? You think I'm cheap? God damn it, all I wanted to do was save the picture."

"We're allies then," Steve said. "Because that's all I want to do, too." He finished his drink. "Thanks a lot, Harry. I knew you'd be reasonable."

"Don't soap me," Bergdahl said. "Fight me but don't soap me. I'll see you later."

Outside, Jean D'Arcy was sitting in Dave's MG, which was parked on the circular drive near the kitchen. Steve went over.

"Aren't you permitted in the house?" he asked jestingly.

"Not today. What's going on in there? I could hear the shouting way out here."

"Story conference," Steve said. "When did Dave come?"

"About fifteen minutes ago. Just before the shouting. He told me he'd be right out. Now, why didn't he invite me in?"

"I've no idea. Your friend Morton is a good friend of Pat Cullum's, I understand."

She studied him. "Why did you say that? Mitch *despises* Pat Cullum. I'll bet that's what you were waiting to hear. You were being tricky, weren't you?"

"No, I was being serious. I thought he dated her."

She shook her head vehemently. "Not Mitch. Tom Leslie now—Pat is exactly the kind of dish Tom is always looking for."

"Tom and every other red-blooded male. Why do you dislike Pat so much?"

"I'm not sure," she said honestly. "Probably because she'll get further with her bust than the rest of us will with our small talents."

Then Dave was there. He looked at Steve and asked, "Well . . . ?"

"We go up tomorrow. I wanted two days but settled for one. Dave, don't fight him. He's a very tough pro, and you're still an amateur."

"I'll fight for my script," Dave said. "He doesn't scare me. I'll fight anybody for my script."

Jean D'Arcy smiled at Steve. "Does he scare you, Mr. Leander?"

Steve said lightly, "I have a wife and two children and a number of oppressive financial obligations. Practically everything and everybody scares me these days."

He left them, faintly annoyed, as usual. Dave would fight for his script, being single and related to a producer. Dave didn't have a script worth fighting for, he thought, until I practically rewrote it.

Easy now, Leander. Don't let a bruised ego embitter you. The young can be innocently unkind.

He drove away remembering the fine, firm breasts of Dotty Bergdahl. He had no urge to go home and face the cool reserve of his wife. He searched his wallet for the card Tomkevic had given him. From a drugstore he phoned the investigator.

He was informed that Mr. Tomkevic was out but would be back in an hour. Steve left his number and drove home.

Marcia wasn't there, and Mrs. Burke didn't know where she had gone. Steve went into the study, restless at his enforced inactivity. Once he started a picture, delays nettled him. Harry could have arranged to do some shooting at the studio today, and Steve wondered why he hadn't.

It had been a quick and unexpected decision Harry had made last night. Steve thought of Dotty's concern. It was possible that something beyond money was bothering Bergdahl. What would be more important than money to Harry?

Jail?

In the papers, there had been no more mention of the unidentified man who had been seen at the top of the bluff. Perhaps it had only been the meaningless remark of a neighbor, and the newspapers had blown it up for its mystery value.

One thing seemed certain. It was time to convince Mitchell Morton he should reveal the name of Jameson's companion on the fatal night. If the girl was innocent, there was no reason for her to stay unidentified. Unless, of course, she had seen or heard something that put her in danger of reprisal. That kind of fear would be strong motivation to stay silent. Who would she fear?

Mitchell Morton feared Harry Bergdahl. He had admitted that. Did his unnamed friend, too? In all the theories, the paths of suspicion seemed to lead back to Harry.

Harry had said he didn't know Morton. Yet Tomkevic had claimed he did and wondered why Morton hadn't gone to him for the job. Jameson had strongly implied that keeping him out of the picture and faking an accident had been Harry's idea. And Dotty had told him that something serious was bothering her husband.

They didn't need the insurance money now. They could get money enough to finish the picture through John Abbot. Steve asked himself, *Is that why I've turned moral?* He had gone investigating *before* John's call last night, he reminded himself, and felt properly noble.

The phone rang and it was Tomkevic. Steve asked, "Are you sure Mitchell Morton had a date with the Cullum girl last night?"

"I'm sure. Jealous, Leander?"

"Not very. But I heard today that Morton despised the girl."

"So? She could still have her uses, I imagine."

"They went out? He didn't only stay a short while?"

"They went out and got drunk. What's bothering you about it?"

"Something I didn't tell you about Morton."

"I'm waiting to hear it."

"Could you come here? Or could I come over to your office?"

"What's wrong with telling me over the phone?"

"I need some time to think, Mr. Tomkevic. I could give it to the police, but I don't want any innocent people smeared. I'll expect some promises from you."

117

A silence of a few seconds and then Tomkevic said, "I have to be in that neighborhood anyway, this afternoon. I'll be at your house in half an hour."

Steve was eating lunch when Tomkevic came. He said, "Sit down and have some coffee. Or eat, if you haven't."

"I'll have some coffee," Tomkevic said. "I've eaten." He sat down.

Steve said, "You'd look very big to your boss, I suppose, if you saved the company a quarter of a million dollars."

"I look big to my boss right now. I'm not out to prove anything that isn't true, Mr. Leander."

Steve smiled at him. "But you told me truth comes out of turbulence. You're out to stir up turbulence, aren't you?"

Tomkevic returned Steve's smile and didn't answer.

"There are some young people involved in this," Steve went on. "Scandal could stop their careers before they were properly started. I'm expecting a high degree of discretion from you."

"I'm sorry. I can't promise that."

"All right, Mr. Tomkevic, enjoy your coffee. Because that's all you'll be getting from me."

"Perhaps the police could get more."

"Perhaps. And perhaps not. I'd be sure to tell them how you tried to blackmail me."

Tomkevic stared. "I—what . . . ? Are you crazy?"

"I'd tell them simply what you told me, that you had planned to tell my wife I had taken Miss Cullum home from a party. I'd tell them it was perfectly innocent but might not look that way to my wife, who was out of town at the time. I'd tell all my friends in the industry about it, too. Your firm gets a lot of studio business, I understand."

Tomkevic continued to stare, his face rigid.

118

Steve asked, "Isn't Donald Allison on your board of directors?"

Tomkevic nodded.

"I know Don very well," Steve said.

Tomkevic's voice was softer than usual. "Are you trying to frighten me? Or impress me? You're not making it."

"I'll quit, then," Steve said. "More coffee?"

Silence. Tomkevic seemed to be breathing more heavily than usual.

Steve said, "Personally, I would benefit if the insurance money was never paid. Because Mr. Bergdahl might then be in financial trouble, and I'm in a position to take advantage of that."

Tomkevic smiled. "Really? My information doesn't show your financial position to be that sound."

"I'll be getting the money through a man named John Abbot," Steve explained. "He's one of my closest friends. You could check that statement and check Mr. Abbot's credit at the same time."

Tomkevic shook his head slowly. "You fooled me, mister. You're a real tough son-of-a-bitch, aren't you?"

"Basically," Steve said lightly, "I'm an artist. But in my trade there are times when it's necessary to be a real tough son-of-a-bitch. I don't suppose you ever have a need to be anything else."

Silence again and Tomkevic finally said, "Maybe. Maybe now would be a good time for me to turn into a diplomat."

"Try one of those rolls," Steve said. "They're very good."

THIRTEEN

He went back to the beginning, to Wednesday, and told Tomkevic everything but the reason for his trip to Jameson's apartment. Silence on the rumor was a half-lie he still owed to Harry Bergdahl, and he had no compunction about not repeating it.

When he had finished, Tomkevic said, "It's simple enough. I go up against Morton. If he refuses to tell me who the girl is, he'll have to answer to the police."

"He's a stubborn man."

Tomkevic said nothing.

Steve asked, "Did you check that Brown, from Tucson?"

"Our Phoenix office is going to check on it today." He stood up. "Well, I'll talk to Morton. I'll take it easy."

"Good luck," Steve said. "You'll—keep me informed, won't you?"

Tomkevic smiled wryly. "Of course, Mr. Leander. I wouldn't want you to report me to your friend, Don Allison."

A good man, Steve thought. An active, perceptive, courageous, efficient man. Earning how much on a job like his? He put in long, tedious hours and probably earned less than a studio electrician.

He went into his study for a nap. His haven, that study, lined with unread books, overlooking the pool and housing the television set. His base of operations, his refuge. *Actually,* he thought, *it's all I need, this one room. The rest is for Marcia and the kids, whether they appreciate it or not.*

Honest, self-sacrificing Steven Leander, one of this area's three great directors, lay on his air-cushioned, soft leather couch, contemplating his essential nobility. It was a fine couch, well worth the fourteen hundred dollars it had cost him. He dozed.

At three o'clock, the phone rang and he picked it up in time to hear the housekeeper tell Tomkevic he was sleeping.

Steve said, "I'm awake. I'll take it, Mrs. Burke."

Tomkevic waited for the extension to click before he said, "That Morton's not home. He's out at Zuma Beach. I'll get him tonight. We got word from Phoenix, though."

"And . . . ?"

"This Edward Ambrose Brown in Tucson is a chemist. He came to work in Tucson a year ago. His job application sheet shows his last place of employment as the Dostel Laboratories in Los Angeles."

"And I suppose you went over immediately to see Dostel?"

"Naturally. But he's not there. The man who runs the delicatessen store across the street told me that Dostel told him he was taking a week or two off, roughing it up in Yosemite."

"Isn't anyone in the laboratory? Hasn't he any help?"

"One helper, the delicatessen man told me. But he doesn't know his name and I'm stymied." Tomkevic paused. "Unless we involve the police now and break in to get Dostel's records."

"We don't need the police yet, do we? We can try to get the real customer's name from Miss Cullum, can't we?"

"She isn't home either."

121

"Let's wait," Steve suggested. "Both she and Morton should be home for dinner. It's only a couple of hours."

A second's silence. Then Tomkevic said, "All right. I'll want you along tonight. In the meantime, I'll try to get the name of Dostel's current employee from the unemployment people."

Steve hung up and went back to sit on the couch. There was nothing unusual about Pat Cullum and Morton not being home, but Dostel's sudden vacation was suspicious. It seemed logical he would have left someone in charge of the business.

He had lied last night. That would indicate he had been forewarned. But who had known that Steve had recognized the perfume? He had told Dave he would remember it and he had accused Pat of wearing it. Pat was the only person who knew Steve had learned the name of the perfume's maker.

Had she warned Dostel? That seemed unlikely. She had called Dostel a liar when Steve had told her about the fictitious customer. Dostel could be trying blackmail. It had been a mistake to mention murder last night. He had gone at Dostel badly. He had blundered in his approach to the man.

He was sunning himself next to the pool when Marcia came home at five o'clock. She stood on the sundeck above, looking down at him, and he sensed that she had something on her mind.

Then she called down, "Shall I mix you a drink?"

He looked up, startled at the change. "Please," he said.

Five minutes later she came down the steps with a pitcher of martinis and two glasses. She poured a pair on the rocks and sat near him in an aluminum and plastic chair.

"I had lunch with Ellen," she said.

Here we go, he thought, *here we go* . . . He said mildly, "That's nice. How is she?"

"The same. She—asked me to ask you if you knew a Pat Cullum."

Steve smiled. "And how! You'll have to meet her. She's quite a girl."

Marcia stared at him perplexedly. "Ellen doesn't make remarks like that to be sociable. What did she mean?"

"I have no idea," he answered. "I could never understand Ellen. Pat Cullum is a girl who wears the same kind of perfume as the girl I smelled but didn't see in Hart Jameson's apartment the night he was murdered. It's a perfume called Dostel Number 263. Have you ever heard of the Dostel perfumes?"

She nodded. "Individualized, aren't they?"

"Exclusively, according to Mr. Dostel. I went to see him about it last night, and Tomkevic and I have reason to believe he lied to me about who bought that number from him."

"Tomkevic and you . . . ?"

"That's right, the insurance investigator. You remember him, don't you?"

"Yes, but what is your connection with him?"

"He and I," Steve said evenly, "have been working very hard on the strange death of Hart Jameson. Together. There are people who will talk to me who won't talk to Mr. Tomkevic. So he asked me to help him. What did you think I've been doing the last few nights?"

"Steve," she asked, "is that the absolute truth?"

He sipped his drink and looked resigned. "In my wallet, up in my lonely bedroom, is Mr. Tomkevic's card. I would be happy if you would phone him and check my story. And then ask Mrs. Burke who I talked with on the phone two hours ago."

123

"I believe you," she said. "And where did you happen to meet this Pat Cullum?"

"At Harry's party. She was with Dave Sidney. That doesn't automatically make Dave a suspect, because Dave is investigating this strange death, too."

"For heaven's sake, why?"

"Because he wants to know if Harry was in any way responsible. And so do I."

"And you thought it was necessary to keep that information from me. That's what you and Dave have been so secretive about?"

He nodded. "It wasn't a part of my life where I wanted you and the children involved."

She looked at him searchingly. "I know you're a con man when you need to be. You won't be too hurt, I hope, if I don't fall immediately into your arms?"

"I can wait," he said. "It's only been three weeks."

"Two and a half," she corrected him. "And that's another thing that made me suspicious, this apparent sex-discipline of yours."

"*Apparent . . . ?*" He frowned at her. "Suspicious? Of what?"

"Don't be naïve, Steven Leander. Where did you go this morning?"

"To Bergdahl's. Harry had an idea we didn't need any more film from Santa Barbara. He wanted to fake some shots. We fought that out to a compromise. I get one day up there. I wanted two and he didn't want me to go at all. I'll make it a long day, so don't expect me home early tomorrow night."

Marcia stared at him. He smiled at her.

"You and your light touch," she said finally. "The guiltier you've been, the lighter your touch."

"Yes, Your Honor," he said. "I'm sorry, Judge." He held out his glass. "Will you pour me a little more?"

"If I didn't have a case," she went on doggedly, "you'd be furious now, you'd be lividly indignant."

"Never mind another olive," he said amiably. "I saved this one. I'm starting to economize."

She poured him another drink. "I'll find out. Ellen will know."

"If you don't mind a vulgarism," he said, "your friend Ellen doesn't know her ass from third base. Did I ask you where you stormed to Thursday night? Did I check to see if you *really* spent the week end with the kids? Am I going to ask my friend Harry if he knows something evil about you?"

"Your friend Harry, that's a good one."

He smiled tolerantly. "You're pressing. Have another drink."

She shook her head. "I had two at lunch with Ellen."

He leaned back and stretched. "Still on the booze, old Ellen, eh? Harry told me it runs in her family."

She stood up and looked down at him musingly. "You know, when you try to be, you can be the most insufferable creature alive. You haven't heard the last word on this."

He nodded sadly. "That's always the trouble. The last word can always be yours and it can so easily be no. That's your sword."

"Perhaps," she suggested acidly, "this Pat Cullum would be more—available."

"Perhaps," he agreed. "I'll probably be seeing her tonight. Of course, Tomkevic will be along, but maybe he'll go out for a sandwich or something."

"One thing is certain," Marcia said thoughtfully, "the girl must have money if she buys her own perfume."

"She doesn't. Tomkevic and I are trying to learn who buys it for her. Dostel lied about it, as I told you."

From the deck above, Mrs. Burke called down, "It's

125

Mr. Tomkevic again, Mr. Leander. He wants to know if he can pick you up here after dinner."

"Tell him I'll be waiting," Steve said.

Mrs. Burke went back into the house and Marcia looked doubtfully at Steve. Then she said quietly, "Be careful tonight, won't you? Promise?"

"I promise," he said solemnly.

As he steered the green Pontiac along Sunset, Tomkevic said, "I figured you could run in and hit that Morton first. You've got a wedge with him; he's in your picture."

"So is Miss Cullum," Steve told him, "since last night. Do you know that they're both home?"

"No."

Steve asked, "Did you find out the name of Dostel's helper?"

"I did. And he's out of town, too. Real strange, isn't it?"

"Everybody's running," Steve said. "I knew the minute I got on this case the action would start."

Tomkevic chuckled and shook his head. "Man, you certainly have changed attitudes since last week. Come into some money or something?"

"I made a moral decision," Steve said smugly.

"To stay out of that Cullum girl's bed?"

"There's no need to be vulgar, Mr. Tomkevic."

The Pontiac turned right, heading into Brentwood, toward the same section of Brentwood where Hart Jameson had lived. In front of a two-story, weathered-stucco apartment building, Tomkevic parked behind Morton's Plymouth.

"Jameson lived only a block from here," Steve said.

"That's right. Coincidence?"

Steve didn't answer.

Tomkevic said, "Explain to him that if this thing

can't be handled quietly, the police will be called in. Well, I guess you'll know what to say."

Steve shrugged and stepped from the car. In the open lobby the mailboxes informed him that Mitchell Morton occupied apartment 6B. That was on the second floor, and Steve walked up the outside staircase.

There was the same kind of mechanical door chime there had been on Jameson's door, and he turned it.

Mitchell Morton came to the door in swimming trunks and terry-cloth jacket. He stared at Steve in surprise.

Steve asked, "May I come in?"

"Of course. I'm sorry . . ." He stepped aside. "Something about the picture?"

Steve came into a small, cluttered living room. "No. About the girl you're protecting. Is it Pat Cullum?"

Morton shook his head slowly. "What made you think that? She's no friend of mine."

"You had a date with her last night. You went out and got drunk together."

Morton opened his mouth—and closed it. He stared at Steve doubtfully.

Steve said, "She wears the same perfume as the girl you're protecting. It's a special perfume and we—and I'm running down the buyer now."

Morton took a deep breath. "You started to say 'we.'"

"I made a mistake. Who was the girl, Morton?"

Morton looked at Steve steadily. "I don't know. I just used that gimmick to blackmail you. I lied to you."

Steve shook his head. "You couldn't. How would you know Hart Jameson and I talked about something which you claimed the girl overheard, something I wouldn't want repeated?"

"Hart told me long before you went to see him that he was planning an accident. Hell, it was no secret."

"You still wouldn't *know* that was why I went to see him."

"I could guess," Mitchell said, "and I did. And I was lucky." He swallowed. "I suppose I'm out of the picture now."

"This has nothing to do with the picture. But I'll have to tell the police what you told me that night at your house."

"Tell them that I blackmailed you?" Disbelief was apparent on Morton's face. "How could that do either of us any good? I swear to you that I'll tell the police exactly what I told you tonight."

"Was it Jean D'Arcy?" Steve asked.

"I don't know who it was. That's my story, Mr. Leander. From now until I die."

"You're being very foolish," Steve said harshly. "You can't afford this kind of foolishness."

Morton met Steve's gaze. "Yes, I can. I don't owe anybody in the world a dime."

"Do you want to tell me why you took Pat Cullum out last night?"

Morton shook his head. "No more than you want to tell me why you took her home from Mr. Bergdahl's party."

"I took her home because I recognized her perfume. And also because she asked me to take her home."

"You don't owe me an explanation," Morton said.

"How did you know I took her home from the party?"

"She told me last night."

"Did she tell you anything else you want to tell me?"

"She told me she had a small bit in the picture, and she told me what you said about her perfume."

"Did she tell you who bought it for her?"

"No."

"I don't imagine, at four hundred dollars an ounce, she bought it for herself."

Morton shrugged. "I know very little about her."

"All right," Steve said. "Good night, Mr. Morton." He turned irritatedly and went out.

In the car Tomkevic listened to the story and said, "Maybe somebody got to him. That's the way it sounds to me. But who?"

"Have you checked him? Do you know where he was the night that Jameson died?"

Tomkevic nodded. "He was out with that D'Arcy girl. They went up to Pasadena to see a play."

Steve asked, "Do we have to go to the police now? I threatened Morton with that."

Tomkevic said dryly, "The Department isn't anxious to get into it, not yet. Not until I can almost wrap it up for them." He tapped the steering wheel and stared out at the street. "Have you noticed where all the fingers point in this mess?"

"You tell me."

"I don't have to. Toward Harry Bergdahl." He turned to face Steve. "Right?"

Steve said, "Harry has a reputation for being tricky. But I'm sure he's no murderer. For that matter, there's been no evidence of murder established."

"Not yet," Tomkevic admitted. "But I think you'll agree there has been considerable evidence of trickery established." He started the engine. "Well, we'll see what luck you have with the Cullum girl."

They had no luck there. Her apartment was dark and there was no answer to Steve's ring.

Tomkevic said wearily, "I've had enough for today. I've been going since eight o'clock this morning. We'll come here again. Tomorrow morning I'll see if there's some way I can get into that laboratory without involving the police."

"Some crooked way?" Steve asked.

"Some way. If I hadn't promised you I'd be discreet, it would be easy."

Steve lighted a cigarette. "Actually, with all your running around, you're no closer to proving murder than when you started, are you?"

"Murder? Probably not. But the possibility of collusion grows stronger, doesn't it? Is murder the only crime that would motivate your helping me?"

"Probably," Steve admitted quietly. "I'm not a policeman."

"You're a citizen, aren't you?" Tomkevic turned back toward Sunset.

Steve didn't answer. He was thinking of tomorrow, planning the day, hoping his cast would be at their Friday level so this morning's compromise from Harry would not be wasted.

As Tomkevic pulled up in front of Steve's house, he told him, "I'll wait until tomorrow night to see Miss Cullum. Will you be able to go alone?"

"I'll try. Tomorrow is going to be a full day."

"And that D'Arcy girl, too," Tomkevic added. "I'd like to have you talk to her."

Steve stared at the detective. "You don't think she's involved in any of this, do you?"

"She's a good friend of Morton's. And of Bergdahl's nephew, too. And she was a friend of Jameson's. What makes her special?"

Steve smiled. "I don't know. I suppose you're right. I like to think she's special. I'll see you tomorrow probably."

"I hope so. You've been a big help."

Steve watched the Pontiac go down the hill and stood on the front lawn for a few minutes after it disappeared, looking out at the light-dotted hills and the illuminated curve of the bay.

It was quiet and peaceful here, but all around him was the city. A big, noisy, complex, struggling, hating, frightened city. He had forgotten, up on his hill, that all of them at all the levels were secretly afraid of tomorrow.

That was their terrifying unknown—tomorrow. And Harry Bergdahl's. And his.

He went into the house. Marcia was in the kitchen, making cinnamon toast. "I got this sudden and ridiculous urge for some," she explained. "Do you think I might be pregnant?"

He smiled. "Maybe. Miss Cullum wasn't home. I think I'll go to bed. Big day tomorrow."

She smiled and said, "Good night."

He didn't fall asleep immediately. He lay in the dark room, remembering her smile.

And he wasn't at all surprised, half an hour later, to hear her open the door quietly and ask, "Too tired . . . ?"

"Never," he assured her. "Not for you. You're one of my favorites."

FOURTEEN

In the morning she had breakfast with him. And when Dave came, she insisted he join them for a cup of coffee.

Dave said teasingly, "I'm glad we're all friends again. What did you buy her, a mink?"

"Marcia isn't interested in material things," Steve answered. "She's never had to be."

She glanced between them and said nothing.

Dave said, "I talked with Tom Leslie yesterday. He's ashamed of himself. For complaining to Uncle Harry, I mean. He asked me to tell you that."

"Is he afraid to tell me directly?"

Dave shrugged. "I wouldn't blame him. You've been a hard man to get along with this past week."

It was Wednesday. Last Wednesday Hart Jameson had died. And because he had died, this was going to be a better picture. Tom Leslie would make it one.

There was a new suspect for the suspicious Tomkevic. From the vantage point of now, Tom Leslie had more reason than any of them to kill Jameson. More reason than any of them, he corrected himself, except Harry Bergdahl.

It was a good day. Steve started it with a short speech, apologizing for any excessive rudeness of his on Monday, and he told them that today was important and their performances would decide its length.

132

They came back to their Friday level, and it didn't turn out to be a long day after all. Again it was Leslie who pulled them up, drawing from them performances to match his own, which was flawless.

In the car, as they waited for Dave, Laura asked, "How were we, Steve?"

"Perfect. I wasn't joking, Laura, when I said this would start a new career for you."

She sighed and smiled and relaxed in the seat.

Then Dave was coming toward the car and he looked troubled. He glanced at Laura before telling Steve, "Uncle Harry wants you to stop at his house on the way home."

"Okay. You look worried."

"I am," Dave said anxiously. "He sounded drunk, Steve. And indignant."

What now, what now, *what now* . . . ?

Dave got into the car. "It's probably about expenses. I can't see him getting mad about anything else."

Laura said nothing but she was no longer smiling and no longer relaxed. She sat silently staring out through the windshield almost all the way home.

When they dropped her, she said, "Watch your temper, won't you, Steve?"

He winked at her. "Yes, mama. I'll see you tomorrow."

As he cut back into the traffic, Steve said, "There's no point in taking you to your car first. You may as well come along."

"He wants me there," Dave said. "I guess he's mad at me, too."

"You don't think it's a relapse from our argument with him yesterday?"

"It could be. He might have got drunk and began to look back on it with a drunk's belligerence. He never used to drink like he has lately. What could be happening to him, Steve?"

"The same thing that's happening to all of us. We're insecure. We're scared. It's a bad time for the industry."

"Hell, there's always TV."

"For you and young Leslie and Morton and your girl, maybe. Not for Harry and me. Our own trade is ridiculous enough; this new one needs younger nerves. Harry and I aren't the type who can kowtow to sponsors and hucksters."

"You and Harry . . . ? You're the same type?"

"In the most important relationship, we're blood brothers."

Dave asked lightly, "And what's the important relationship, Uncle Steve?"

"Belief," Steve answered quietly. "We believe in our medium."

Dotty opened the front door for them. She said softly, "He's in the living room. He's drunk." She walked ahead of them into the provincial living room.

Harry sat in a big chair near the fireplace, sweating, scowling and obviously drunk. He stared at Steve, transferred the stare to Dave and then brought it back to Steve.

He said, "Leave, Dotty. This is business."

"I want to stay. If Dave can stay, I can."

He turned his head slowly to look at her. "Dave is not here as my nephew. Go, now."

For seconds she met his gaze, then turned and left the room.

Harry looked back at them. "You're a pair. Detectives, huh? Nosing around, trying to pin something on Harry. That will be the day."

Steve said gently, "Neither Dave nor I are trying to pin anything on you, Harry. If you were sober, you wouldn't talk like this."

134

"Stirring up the cast," Harry accused him. "Slowing up the picture." He glared at Steve. "Why? You think you can get money from Abbot and buy me out?"

Steve shook his head. "That's absurd and you know it, Harry. You're not making sense to me, and I'm sure you aren't to Dave, either."

"You're thinking for him now? He's your nephew now?" He stared at Dave. "That Cullum girl—she's a friend of yours?"

Dave shook his head.

Harry asked, "But the D'Arcy girl, maybe?"

Dave nodded. "A good friend. I'm hoping she'll be more than that. What's wrong with her, Uncle Harry?"

"You tell me. She's in the picture all of a sudden. Morton's in the picture. Now the Cullum girl. Jameson's friends. Maybe they all told you something and you paid them off that way, huh?"

Steve looked at Dave and then went over to sit on the davenport. "Harry," he said evenly, "I don't know exactly what you're getting at, but if you're talking about Jameson's brag, that's the worst-kept secret in town. It's why I went over to see him last Wednesday night. And it's why Tomkevic hasn't given up on this case. But neither Dave nor I had anything to do with starting or spreading that rumor."

"Who started it then?"

"Jameson, with his bragging at a party. And when I went to see him, he practically told me this accident he had planned was your idea."

"And you told Tomkevic that?"

"No."

Harry squinted suspiciously. "You've been riding around with him. You've been working with him."

"Yes. But I didn't tell him what Jameson told me and I never will."

135

Silence. Dave said, "Jameson was a bad man to confide in, Uncle Harry. He was all mouth."

Harry sat without speaking, breathing heavily, glaring at both of them.

Steve asked, "Who told you I'd been working with Tomkevic?"

"What difference does it make? Don't worry, I got friends with eyes and ears. You know you damned near scared off my angel? But you didn't make it. You were trying to scare off my money, weren't you?"

"Of course not," Steve said sharply. "I thought that money was firm."

Harry sneered. "Firm . . . ? That's some word. What does it mean? When you've spent it and they ain't got grounds to sue you, then it's firm. You talk like a real-estate peddler. Firm—*Jesus!*"

There was a silence, broken only by the sound of Harry's heavy breathing. Then Dave said, "I'll get my car later, Steve. I'll stay here for dinner."

Harry glared at his nephew. "I don't need you here for dinner. Who asked you?"

"I'd like to stay, Uncle Harry. I'd really like to try to explain a lot of things to you."

For a moment, Harry's glare seemed to dim. Finally, he said grudgingly, "Maybe it's about time." He looked at Steve. "We'll talk some more later. We'll talk straight."

Steve nodded. He left without another word.

A new alliance, Dave and Harry against him? Or an old alliance reëstablished? He stilled the thought; he was beginning to think like Harry. To Harry, all who weren't one-hundred percent with him were enemies.

At home Marcia said, "You're earlier than I expected. Where's Dave?"

"At Harry's." Steve told her about the scene in Harry's living room.

She shook her head and said nothing.

"He was drunk," Steve explained. "Drunk and belligerent. He'll be more reasonable when he sobers up."

She nodded absently. She stared at Steve. "You know I'm not in his fan club. But can you see him as a murderer?"

"No. Though I couldn't say why."

"I can't either," she said. "Oh—Mr. Tomkevic phoned and said he'd pick you up about eight-thirty." She made a face. "He wants you along when he visits Miss Cullum."

"I suppose I'd better go." He rubbed the back of his neck. "I could use a drink."

She patted his cheek gently. "I'll bring you one. Sit down and relax."

As he sat there, waiting for his drink, he thought of Harry's scorn for the word "firm." It was a new scorn; Harry had used exactly that word when he had first talked with Steve. Perhaps the Texan had definitely backed out. Perhaps Harry had lied about that. It was strange that the Texan hadn't been at the cast party.

At eight o'clock Dave came for his car. Dotty had driven him over and she told Steve that Harry was asleep.

Marcia said sweetly, "Then why don't you and Dave stay here and visit with me for a while? Steve has to go out this evening."

Dotty looked pleased and surprised. Dave smiled at Steve. Steve kissed his wife and murmured in her ear, "Don't get too nice. It's out of character." He went out front to wait for Tomkevic. Perhaps, if he caught him in front, Dave wouldn't see him.

He didn't tell the investigator about this afternoon's session with Harry. He asked him if he had been able to locate Dostel or his assistant.

"No, but I did send a list of names to the Phoenix

office, and our man there will go to Tucson to see if that Brown recognizes any of them as Dostel customers. Of course, he's been gone from here for a year."

"And he probably wouldn't remember the numbers if he should remember the names."

"Maybe not. But it will be another wedge." He turned toward the Palisades. "I want you to see the D'Arcy girl first tonight. See if you can shake her alibi for Morton."

"You mean, you think they didn't go to Pasadena that night?"

"It's highly doubtful. I checked for that night, and the house was sold out for a P.T.A. benefit. The lady I talked to up there this morning swears that every seat was sold to Pasadena residents two days before the presentation. Morton and the girl probably saw the play together some other night and decided it would make a good alibi."

"I can't see Jean D'Arcy as a liar."

"How about Morton? All his friends claim he's a real square joe. But he tried to blackmail you, didn't he?"

Steve said quickly, "I never told you that."

"You damned near told me that. You will, eventually."

Steve smiled. "You still don't trust me, do you?"

"Should I, completely? Think before you answer."

Steve thought—and didn't answer. The Pontiac went drumming along toward the Palisades.

Tomkevic said, "Remember now, unless Morton and the girl were somebody's guests, they didn't see the show that night. And if they were somebody's guests, I want the name of their host. That woman is sending me the entire reservation list."

"Tiger, tiger," Steve murmured.

"What's that?"

"Nothing," Steve said. "You certainly are a hard worker, aren't you?"

"And I deal with such miserable people," Tomkevic added. "Present company excepted, of course."

The apartment building was on Sunset, west of the Palisades shopping district. Tomkevic pulled around the corner and told Steve, "Remember, now, it's Morton's alibi you're checking. If you make her realize she's not under suspicion, you'll be likely to get more honest answers."

The apartment was on the first floor, on the corner, and there was the sound of music coming from an open window as Steve went past it to the door.

The sound of the music stopped before she opened the door. She looked at Steve in perplexity. "Well . . . ! Didn't you bring a bottle? Isn't that the standard opening gambit?"

"You overestimate your charms," he told her. "I came for information."

She flushed faintly, staring at him. Then she said quietly, "Come in."

He came into a small, uncarpeted and sparsely furnished living room. The record player was on a card table in one corner. Another card table was set for dinner.

Steve stood right inside the still open doorway and said, "I came to check on Mitchell Morton. He claims to have been with you last Wednesday night."

"He was. We went to the Pasadena Playhouse."

"Not Wednesday night. All the seats were reserved, and there is no record of your reservations."

She frowned. "The seats are reserved every night. But tickets can be bought at the box office, and there would be no record of who bought them."

"You mean he didn't reserve the seats in advance?"

139

"That's right. He bought two reserved seats when we got there."

Steve shook his head. She stared at him.

Steve said, "Last Wednesday night all the seats were sold before the box office opened. It was a P.T.A. benefit, and we have the listing of every purchaser."

"We . . . ?" She licked her lips. "Who did you mean by 'we'? Why are you checking me? What right have you to investigate me?"

"No right," Steve answered. "But to save all of you from being investigated by the police, I'm working with the insurance-company investigator on the death of Hart Jameson."

"To save all of *us?* Who do you mean by that?"

"At the moment, I mean you and Mitchell Morton."

"Nonsense," she said hoarsely. "What are we to you? Why should you want to save us from anything?"

"It's complicated," he told her gently. "But believe me, I do."

"I've nothing to fear from the police," she said. "You have my permission to stop protecting me from them. Good night, Mr. Leander."

"You're being foolish."

She smiled thinly. "Good night. I don't need that part. Don't slam the door."

"This has nothing to do with the part," he told her. "And you're not under suspicion. It's Morton's alibi I'm concerned with."

"And Mitch is my best friend. Will you go?"

He nodded. "I'll go. Ask your best friend how he happened to get *his* part in the picture. Ask him to tell you the truth, if it's in him."

"Go, *please!*" she whispered. Her chin quivered.

He went out and down to the car. Tomkevic looked at him questioningly.

140

"I feel like a twenty-two-karat bastard," Steve said. "But you didn't learn anything."

"Nothing. She's being loyal to Morton. Is that a crime?"

Tomkevic shrugged. "I don't know. If Jameson was murdered, it's a crime."

Steve said grimly, "There's not the slightest goddamned shred of evidence that Jameson was murdered. Actually, there's just your two hundred and fifty thousand-dollar motivation for wanting the accident to look like a murder."

Tomkevic smiled. "You're beginning to hate me again. Either me or your conscience. Does this mean you don't want to go over and see the Cullum girl with me?"

"That's right. I'd tackle Morton with you. But no more women, no more lambs."

"Morton isn't home. Look, Leander, let's run over to see the Cullum girl, and then I'll take you home. Then, if you want to drop out of further participation, I'll take what I have, and what I intend to get, to the police. And your lousy lambs can go up against some real wolves. Okay?"

"Okay," Steve said wearily. "Now you're hot. Why?"

"Your bleeding heart. Your great compassion for liars and blackmailers and whores. If you want to bleed for worth-while people, Leander, the town is loaded with them. And not a single one of them has a Guild card."

"Don't lecture me," Steve said. "You're not qualified. Drive on, Hawkshaw."

They had no further words for each other on the long trip to the apartment building that housed Pat Cullum. There Steve said curtly, "I'll wait in the car."

Tomkevic turned to stare at him for seconds before

getting out and going up the walk. There was, Steve saw, no light visible in the windows of the girl's apartment.

Tomkevic disappeared around the turn of the stairs, and Steve lighted a cigarette. In about a minute Tomkevic came down the steps again, but he didn't come to the car. He went to an apartment on the first floor and rang the bell.

A few seconds of conversation and then Tomkevic and the man who had answered the door went up the steps together. Steve watched the windows of Pat Cullum's apartment and saw the light go on.

Apprehension moved through him, and he watched the steps anxiously. A few minutes later Tomkevic and the man came down. The man went into his apartment, and Tomkevic came down to the car.

He didn't get in. He stood on the curb and said woodenly, "We'll wait here for the police. One of your lambs is dead, and this time I know it wasn't an accident. She was murdered, stabbed to death."

FIFTEEN

In a small and dreary room in the Hollywood station, Steve and Tomkevic waited for Sergeant Morrow. He worked out of Headquarters, but he had been called after Tomkevic had explained the connection between Hart Jameson's death and Pat Cullum's.

Steve had phoned Marcia. Dave and Dotty had still been there. Dave was on his way down to the station.

Tomkevic smoked a cigar and stared at the floor. He didn't look at Steve. There had been very few words between them since their angry words in front of Jean D'Arcy's apartment.

A detective came in to tell Tomkevic, "She's been dead about ten hours, as close as we're able to figure so far. Does that ring any bells with you?"

Tomkevic shook his head. "That would make it around one o'clock. I don't know what any of them were doing at that time. How about her neighbors?"

"They're being checked now." He glanced at Steve and then moved closer to Tomkevic. He began to speak quietly, too quietly for Steve to hear.

Steve lighted a cigarette. He was not a heavy smoker, but he had been smoking constantly since the discovery of Pat Cullum's death. His mouth was dry, his throat irritated.

The door opened and a uniformed man came in.

143

Jean D'Arcy was with him. She looked exceptionally young and frightened, standing next to the big policeman, staring bewilderedly at Steve.

Steve rose and went over to ask her, "Would you like a lawyer, Jean? I'll phone mine, if you want."

The uniformed man said, "Let the little lady do her own thinking, mister. We'll inform her of her rights."

Jean said, "I don't need a lawyer. I don't need anything from you, Mr. Leander."

The detective came over then. "Miss D'Arcy?"

She nodded.

"I want to talk to you and Mr. Tomkevic in another room." He looked at Steve. "You wait here." He turned to the uniformed man. "How about that Morton?"

"Ebey is looking for him now, Sergeant. He wasn't home, hasn't been home all day."

Steve went back to sit on the hard chair near the window. Dave would be surprised to find his true love here when he arrived. Or perhaps he wouldn't. Maybe Dave knew more about everything that had happened than anyone in this room.

They were all going out when Sergeant Morrow came in. Tomkevic talked with him for a moment at the door and then Tomkevic left with the others and Morrow came over to the small desk in one corner of the room.

He said, "Bring your chair over here, Mr. Leander." He sat down behind the desk.

Steve brought the chair over and sat where he would be facing the officer.

Morrow glanced through some papers on his desk and then looked up at Steve. "You weren't honest with me last time we talked, were you?"

"Yes. What makes you think I wasn't, Sergeant?"

"We'll get to that. Consider it from my angle. So far as we know, you were the last man to see Hart Jameson alive. Tonight you discover the body of this Cullum girl. What would you think, sitting where I am?"

"I don't know, Sergeant. I didn't discover the body of Miss Cullum. Mr. Tomkevic did."

"You were along."

Steve nodded.

"Why?"

Steve frowned. "Why not?"

"You're a director, aren't you? You're not an investigator. At least you're not licensed as an investigator."

"Mr. Tomkevic thought I might be helpful to him. The death of Hart Jameson bothered me and I wanted to help."

"Why should it bother you? We had about written it off as an accident."

"Not *about*. You *had* written it off as an accident. Tomkevic wasn't satisfied with that decision and he asked me to help him. I'm sure he'll tell you I was a help."

Sergeant Morrow asked, "And did you withhold from him, as you did from us, the real reason you went to see Hart Jameson on the night he died?"

"Withhold what?" Steve asked. "What do you think my real reason was for visiting him?"

"To try to talk him into faking an accident."

Steve said heatedly, "That's not true. Nothing could be further from the truth than that."

Morrow's smile was cynical. "You'd swear to that under oath?"

"I certainly would. Now, or in court."

"You'll probably get the chance. Well, an officer should be in here any minute to take your statement. You can go, after that."

Steve nodded.

Morrow said, "I'm going easy on you, at the moment, because Mr. Tomkevic told me you'd been very help-

145

ful. But you're not out of the woods by a long shot. Give it a lot of thought, Mr. Leander, and I'm sure you'll realize complete frankness is your best course now."

Steve nodded again.

Dave arrived before the stenographer came in. He seemed nervous and his voice was high. "Where's Jean?"

"I don't know. She went to another room with Tomkevic and a detective. How did you know she was down here?"

"The desk sergeant told me."

There was a silence, and then Dave asked, "Why did you go to see her tonight?"

"To find out why she lied about Morton. Your girl's in trouble, Dave, and not because of me. She would have saved herself a lot of trouble, though, if she hadn't lied to me."

Dave's chin came up. "I don't believe she lied. I'm getting her a lawyer. They won't push her around."

"How did you know I went to see her tonight?"

Dave took a deep breath. "I phoned her from your house, right after you'd been there. You're not a policeman, Steve, or an investigator."

"I stayed with it longer than you did," Steve said quietly. "What made you quit so suddenly, Dave?"

Dave started to say something and then stopped. He asked plaintively, "Why are we fighting? This is—embarrassing to me."

"And to me," Steve admitted. "But, Dave, tell your girl she's making a mistake in trying to protect Morton. He's not at all what she thinks he is. He tried to blackmail me last Thursday night."

Dave stared, his mouth open. "Mitchell Morton . . . ?"

"That's right. He phoned to tell me he knew the girl who had been in Jameson's apartment and she overheard what Jameson and I were talking about. And now he can't be found. You tell Jean that."

146

Dave shook his head wonderingly. "Why should she want to protect him? What did she lie about?"

"She claimed she went to Pasadena with Morton last Wednesday night. Tomkevic can almost prove she didn't."

"Wednesday night? That's the night Jameson was killed."

"Right."

Dave said slowly, "I know she wasn't with Morton. She had a date with me that night."

"So. And a few minutes ago you said you wouldn't believe she'd lie. Do you now?"

Dave didn't answer.

"And only to protect a man who's not worth it," Steve added. "You'd better find her and give her the word."

An officer came in with a stenographer's notebook as Dave went out. The detective who had been with Tomkevic came in a few minutes later.

Steve asked him, "Have you located Mitchell Morton?"

The detective shook his head. "Why?"

"He seems to be the key, doesn't he? He even went out with Miss Cullum the other night, though I know they weren't friends. Why would he date her?"

"Do you know they weren't friends or is that just something you were told?"

"I was told that by Miss D'Arcy and by Morton himself."

The detective smiled. "I'm sure you don't believe everything that pair tell you. Let's get on with the statement, Mr. Leander."

Steve started with his visit to Jameson's apartment and related all that seemed pertinent, omitting the information that he had first heard the rumor from Laura. The police already had the rumor, through Tomkevic; there was no point in involving Laura.

When he had finished, the detective told him, "Tomkevic will be around here for quite a while yet, but Mr. Sidney told me he'd take you home. He's waiting in the hall."

Jean was in the hall with Dave. Steve said, "We can't all ride in that little bug of yours, can we?"

"I brought Dotty's car," Dave answered. "She took mine home from your house." He smiled at Jean. "Aren't you going to say it?"

She glanced at Dave and then looked steadily at Steve. "Dave thinks I owe you an apology. And I guess I do."

"You don't," he said. "Loyalty is a rare but still admirable virtue."

She continued to look at him steadily. "Even when it's misplaced?"

"Especially then. It's easy to ride with a winner. Let's go home. I'm worn out."

Dave chewed his lip and stared at Steve. "I guess you and I will have a loyalty test soon, too."

Steve looked at him quizzically.

Dave nodded toward a closed door. "The way Tomkevic is shaping things up in there, all the fingers are pointing at Uncle Harry."

"They always did," Steve said dully. "Let's go."

As they rode along in Dotty's convertible, Steve thought of Tomkevic. He had compared him mentally with Javert, but the man was changing into a different image. Tomkevic, despite his unctuous speeches, was less concerned with the law and justice than he was with saving his firm's money.

Steve asked, "Did your uncle know Morton before I gave him that part?"

"I don't think so. Why?"

"Tomkevic claimed he did."

"Tomkevic has made a lot of claims. And he's got reason to."

"That's what I've been thinking. Are you going to stay at your uncle's tonight?"

"I doubt it. Did you want to talk with him?"

"I think both of us should talk with him. But he's probably still sleeping. Well, I'll phone him early in the morning. Or, if he's awake when you go to pick up your car, have him phone me tonight. I'll stay up for a while."

Dave said, "If he's awake, he's probably still drunk. Tomorrow should be soon enough, don't you think?"

"I suppose. Dave, tell him we don't need the damned insurance money. Tell him we can get the money through John Abbot, and Harry will still be boss."

Dave smiled wearily. "Okay, I'll tell him. But you know damned well what he'll tell me."

Steve smiled and didn't answer. Dave was right. Harry Bergdahl had grown up in a world where survival was a tricky business, where proffered friendships needed critical and cynical examination. *Don't do me any favors.* That was the motto on Harry's shield.

At home, Marcia said, "I've made some cocoa. You used to like cocoa after a bad day."

He kissed her. "It's been a good day and a bad evening. Did anyone call? Are we going to work tomorrow?"

"Harry called," she said. "You're not working. He said you shouldn't call him back until tomorrow morning."

"Why not?"

She shrugged. "He didn't say. Steve, have the police learned anything?"

"I don't know. They don't confide in me."

"Harry sounded drunk—drunk and frightened."

149

"He's probably both. Let's get to the cocoa."

She nodded. "And then you soak in a hot bath. And sleep late tomorrow."

The hot bath helped. He lay in it, trying to blank his mind, trying to forget the picture Tomkevic's words had triggered, the mental picture of Pat Cullum in her dark apartment, stabbed to death. He reached one wet hand up to touch his bitten ear. It was almost healed.

SIXTEEN

The morning *Times* had a new development in the murder since Steve had left the Hollywood station. Mitchell Morton had appeared of his own volition at Central Headquarters. He had brought two things with him: a new story and Leon Spangler.

Leon Spangler was the most expensive criminal lawyer in this town of expensive criminal lawyers, and he had never been known to work for charity. That fact was strange enough.

Morton's new story was even stranger. In this new fantasy, he claimed that he had been on his way to see Jameson when he had seen Jameson drive off with a girl. It had been dark and he couldn't be sure of the girl's identity, but he had been *almost* sure that she was Pat Cullum. Jameson was obviously drunk and Morton had followed in his car, remembering the rumor he had heard about Jameson planning an accident.

Jameson, he related, had lost him momentarily on one of the curving streets in the area near the bluff. Then, as he swung around a turn, his headlights had picked up the picture of the Jaguar sliding over the edge of the cliff. And a girl was running along the sidewalk toward another car parked at the curb.

He had not been able to see the driver of the car, he claimed, nor the face of the girl. He had identified the car as an MG. Morton had parked, gone to the edge of the bluff and seen the crumpled car below.

He had been afraid to go to the police. He claimed he had been aware that there were "big-money interests" involved in the planned accident of Jameson, and at this stage in his acting career he could not afford to alienate them. Further than that, on advice of his expensive counsel, deponent said naught.

It was a ludicrously vulnerable story in many ways. It was a very weak story, but Spangler had permitted him to bring it in to the police. It was logical to guess that it was the strongest story Morton could devise out of those elements already known to the police.

Tomkevic had said that truth quite often came out of turbulence. The turbulence had swirled around Mitchell Morton, and there could be some truth, some necessary truth, in his statement.

He could easily have been the unidentified man the police had not been able to uncover. He could have seen Jameson's car go over the cliff. Identifying the waiting car as an MG could be the truth or it could be a red herring. His uncertain identification of Miss Cullum was understandable. If the friends Miss Cullum had been with that night didn't come forward to dispute this story, it would stand. If they did come forward, Morton had not made positive identification.

The statement could explain why he had gone out with Pat Cullum the other night. He could say he had hoped to get her drunk enough to admit she had been the occupant of Jameson's car. With a man of Spangler's cunning staging it for a jury, this could even be believable.

There would be no urgent reason to take Morton to court. His previous lies had not been told to police officers, and he had not told them under oath. Withholding information from the police was his only known crime. He was much more valuable to the police as a witness.

"He's a goddamned liar," Steve said.

Across the table from him, Marcia looked up, startled. "Who is?"

He handed her the paper. When she had finished reading the account, she said hesitantly, "That—part about the MG—didn't Dave bring this Cullum girl to Harry's party?"

"That's right. And Morton was at the party; he knew Dave had brought her. That's what makes that bit look like a red herring to me."

"But why should this Morton want to involve Dave?"

"Because Dave's already involved to some degree. And that makes Morton's lie more plausible." He paused. "If it is a lie.

"How is Dave involved?" he continued. "He brought Pat Cullum to the party. Pat Cullum wore the same perfume as the girl in Jameson's apartment. Dave is Harry's nephew, and Harry took out the insurance policy. It's a real involved deal Mr. Morton has hinted at."

"And you don't believe it?"

"Should I? Who told him I'd visited Jameson? How did he know the girl in the other room overheard us? Who are the big-money interests he's so scared of?"

"Harry Bergdahl?" asked Marcia.

Steve smiled dryly. "Harry would be very pleased right now to be known as a big-money interest. Only he isn't."

Marcia said slowly, "This town is full of MG's. There's nothing unusual about them out here."

"That's right. And Dave has his alibi for that night: Jean D'Arcy. And she has Dave. That forced Morton to change his story and could be another reason why he identified the waiting car as an MG."

153

Marcia poured herself another cup of coffee. She looked at the cup as she said, "Well, anyway, you're not involved. Harry might be, but you're not."

"Look at me," Steve commanded her.

She looked at him.

"I'm involved," he said evenly. "Harry's involved, so I'm involved. Because he took me from the ranks of the unemployed, and let us not forget that for even one second."

"Nonsense," she said. "He needed you. He never would have called you if he hadn't needed you."

"And I needed him even more," Steve answered. "And maybe he needs me now. I'm going over to find out."

Morton had lied. So had Dostel and Jean D'Arcy. Who else had lied? Rather than lie, Pat Cullum had refused to answer. Harry Bergdahl had admitted nothing tangible, but there had been no proof he had lied. Morton, Dostel, D'Arcy—they were amateurs, and lying badly was the mark of amateurs. Leon Spangler was no amateur. Who was paying his fee?

Dave was just getting out of his little black car when Steve drove up in front of Bergdahl's. He waited on the driveway.

Steve said, "I'm surprised you're free after your friend Morton identified the getaway car."

"I've just come from the station," Dave explained. "He's no friend of mine. Or Jean's either, any more."

"Are they holding him?"

Dave shook his head. "Not with Spangler representing him. And will you tell me where the bum got the money to hire expensive help like Leon Spangler?"

"That's a question I should think the police would ask. Do you know if Harry's awake and sober?"

Dave shrugged. "We'll soon know." They walked to the front door and Dave opened it.

154

Somewhere in the house a radio was tuned to a news report, and the commentator was talking about the death of Pat Cullum. Dave led the way to the kitchen.

It was a huge, beamed, farm kitchen, and the breakfast table had been set near the used-brick fireplace. Harry and Dotty were at the table, reading the morning paper.

Dotty smiled in greeting, and her glance rested appraisingly on Steve. Harry said sourly, "The detectives, the investigators."

Dave laughed. Steve said, "We're here to comfort you, Harry. We're here to hold your hand."

Dotty said smilingly, "There's a whole pot of coffee. Get some cups, Dave."

Steve sat down as Dave went to the cupboard. Harry said growlingly, "So what's on your mind?"

"I wondered if you had phoned your lawyer. Tomkevic seems determined to railroad you, Harry."

"That would bother you?"

Steve nodded solemnly.

Harry looked away. "I don't need a lawyer. They rob you blind. What do I need with a lawyer? I'm clean."

Steve said nothing. Dave brought a pair of cups and saucers. Dotty smiled at Steve and winked at Dave.

Harry asked, "Why are you worried? Since when does Steven Leander worry about cornball Harry Bergdahl?"

"Since you gave me a job when I needed it. Do you want me to go, Harry? It's your house."

Dotty said softly, "Harry doesn't know who his real friends are. He doesn't trust anybody." She poured Steve a cup of coffee.

"Friends . . . ?" Harry said bitterly. "Some friends, a pair of suspicious associates, nosing into my business. I can live without friends like that."

Steve said jestingly, "Why worry? You're clean."

155

Harry glared. "A hundred percent clean nobody is. Are you?"

Steve shook his head.

"Nobody working and me paying rent at the studio," Harry went on. "And why . . . ? Tell me, *why?*"

"I don't know, Harry. It was your idea."

"To start all the trouble it was my idea? Oh, no. You and my loving nephew here, it was your idea."

Dave asked, "And whose idea was it to insure Hart Jameson?"

Harry transferred his glare to his nephew. "Mine." He gestured impatiently. "The old days are dead. Now a guy's gotta make pictures with class. That means stepping up publicity about stars, their insurance gimmicks, tough location breaks—all that flapdoodle. You know how the columns like to kick it around." Then more softly, "But the accident idea—that was *his*. He thought we had a dog of a script. He thought it would hurt his nothing reputation."

Steve said, "I wouldn't admit all that to Tomkevic, Harry."

"Was I born yesterday? I'll get to him. His time will come."

Dave asked, "Could I fry myself a couple of eggs, Dotty? I'm starving."

"Ask me," Harry said. "I pay for the eggs around here."

Dotty said sweetly, "I'll fry them for you, Dave. He can take them out of my allowance."

Dave smiled. Steve managed to keep a straight face.

Harry tapped the newspaper. "Did you read this Morton's bull? Who's the big-money interests?"

Dave said mildly, "I wouldn't be surprised if he meant you, Uncle Harry."

Bergdahl nodded. "I never liked that man. I still

think he's on a list somewhere. He's a liar. I'll bet he made a deal with that Polack insurance man."

Steve said soothingly, "Harry, let's not think about anything but the picture. If the insurance money isn't paid, we'll get money somewhere else and you'll still be kingpin. But let's worry about nothing but the picture."

"*Now* you talk like that. After you and Dave mess around for a week with your big noses."

"So we're not messing around any more. I think we should get right back to work tomorrow, and I think Mitchell Morton should still have that part."

Harry stared. "Are you crazy? Is he a buddy of yours or something?"

"I despise him. But he's the man for the part, and we'll get him at minimum. Harry, I said we should think *only* of the picture."

Bergdahl studied him thoughtfully. Finally he said, "You're right. Yeh, you're right. I hope we can get him before he goes to jail. Because that's where he's going to wind up."

Dotty brought the eggs over and Dave began to eat.

Bergdahl was still studying Steve. His chin went up. "You know, I always had the feeling you figured me for a bastard. Maybe I was wrong about that, huh?"

Steve shook his head and smiled. "It's only that I'm beginning to realize you're my kind of bastard, Harry."

Bergdahl's dour face was impassive for a moment and then he also smiled. "We're going to have a picture, ain't we? Nobody's going to stop that."

"We're going to have a picture," Steve promised.

The phone rang and Dotty picked it up. She said, "Yes, he's here." She looked at Steve. "It's for you."

It was Sergeant Morrow. He said, "We got that statement typed up that you dictated last night. You can drop in at the Hollywood station any time today to sign it."

157

"I'll do that, Sergeant. How is it you didn't hold Mitchell Morton? It's obvious from my statement that his story was fabricated, isn't it?"

"It's obvious either his story was fabricated or your statement is fabricated, Mr. Leander. Or maybe both."

"Thanks, Sergeant. Next time I'll know better than to answer a summons for help."

"The summons didn't come from us, Leander."

"You're right, it didn't, Morrow. Good-bye." He replaced the phone on its cradle roughly.

"Temper, temper . . ." Dotty said.

Dave said, "That Morrow can be nasty. If I was twenty pounds heavier, I'd have slugged him this morning."

Harry was doing the smiling now. He said nothing.

Steve said, "I'll go over and sign the statement. And then I think I'll go to the studio and see if I can find anyone there to run yesterday's rushes for me. They should be terrific."

"They'd better be," Harry said. "Because you'll remember we agreed yesterday was your last day up there."

"I remember, skinflint. Now, you call me if Tomkevic sends any law over here. I've got the best attorney in town."

Dave said, "Not for this kind of trouble. Morton's got *him*."

At the Hollywood station, the desk sergeant told him, "Sergeant Morrow has the statement. He's in that first room on the right off the hall."

It was the same room Steve had waited in last night. Sergeant Morrow sat behind the small desk in the corner. He looked up without smiling as Steve walked in.

He nodded at a chair on the other side of the desk. "Sit down, Mr. Leander."

Steve sat down and took out a cigarette.

158

Morrow asked, "Cool off? I've heard about your temper."

Steve didn't answer.

"You've got some reason to hate Mitchell Morton, have you?"

"He's a liar. He's a blackmailer."

"Blackmailed you, did he?"

"Not quite. He was the man for the part and he got it. He's still got it, as far as Mr. Bergdahl and I are concerned. That is, if he's not in jail by the time we get around to shooting it."

"Jail . . . ? What has he done?"

"Withheld information from the police, at the very least."

"So did you, and you're not in jail."

"All right," Steve said vexedly. "You win, Sergeant. It's your baby, not mine. Where's the statement?"

Sergeant Morrow's smile was slight. "You're turning in your badge, are you? Getting out of the investigation business?"

"That's right. And I here and now apologize for letting Tomkevic talk me into it in the first place."

"No need for an apology," Morrow said. "You helped. And now maybe things are getting too hot?"

Steve stared at him. "Is that an accusation? If it is, I'd like to phone my attorney."

Morrow lifted a hand. "Now, take it easy. Nobody's accusing you of anything. It's your boss I was thinking of."

Steve said patiently, "Only because Tomkevic steered your thinking that way. And I'm sure you know why Tomkevic would want Mr. Bergdahl involved."

Morrow nodded. "I considered all that. And I figured Morton for what you called him, a liar and a blackmailer. But a smart liar knows just how much truth to put into his story, and I figure Morton for a smart liar.

159

The parts of his story that check with other stories point directly at Mr. Bergdahl. Right now, we're running down a pretty solid rumor that this Pat Cullum was Bergdahl's girl friend."

"That could be," Steve agreed. "His and any other available male's. At least that was the girl's reputation."

Morrow frowned. "She's dead. Is that a nice way to talk about the dead?"

Steve looked at the unlighted cigarette in his hand and put it absently into his pocket. He looked at Morrow and said nothing.

Morrow said quietly, "I meant Mr. Bergdahl's *special* girl friend, special enough for him to pay her rent. That's the rumor we're running down. Now, what have you got to say?"

"I came here to sign a statement. Where is it?"

"You're being insolent, Mr. Leander."

"I'm trying not to be. Consider this—you and your Department friends wrote off the death of Hart Jameson as an accident. Tomkevic, for financial reasons, and I, for moral reasons, weren't satisfied with that decision. We nosed around. And probably, because of that, Pat Cullum was killed. If we had let it go as an accident, Pat Cullum would probably still be alive and I wouldn't have to sit here and listen to you tell me I'm not out of the woods. I was *way* out of the woods before I turned moral."

"*Turned* moral?"

"Turned actively instead of passively moral. There's a distinction there I'm not sure you're mentally equipped to understand."

"There goes that insolence again."

Steve nodded. "The trouble with you boys is you think a man has to wear a badge to be insolent."

Morrow leaned back in his chair and shook his head.

160

"Jesus, I'd hate to work for you. You must be a real tiger."

Steve said nothing. He put his trembling hands in his lap. Morrow shuffled through some papers and picked out a stapled sheaf of three. He pushed it across to Steve. "There's your statement. Better read it carefully before you sign it."

Steve read it and signed it. Morrow gave him two more copies. "These are carbons."

Steve signed those. He finished and asked, "Assuming you prove that Pat Cullum was Mr. Bergdahl's *special* girl friend. How does that connect him with Jameson's death?"

"She was with Jameson, wasn't she? Maybe working for Bergdahl?"

"She wasn't with Jameson when he died. She told me she went on a double date that night and there would be three witnesses to testify she had been with them."

"Why haven't they come forward? If they can read, they should be here, shouldn't they? And you're overlooking one thing, Leander."

"What's that?"

"Your boss could be innocent of what happened to Jameson and still be guilty of Miss Cullum's death. We haven't been able to prove where he was at the time she died."

"Have you asked him?"

Morrow nodded.

"I just saw him half an hour ago. He didn't tell me that."

Morrow smiled. "You know, there could be a lot of things he hasn't told you. Or us. Thanks for coming in, Mr. Leander."

161

Steve went out into an overcast day and drove to the studio. It was time to concentrate on the important thing, on the picture. He was not a detective and certainly not a lawyer. He had been a writer, was now a director and would one day be a producer. God and TV willing.

He found a projectionist he knew and they ran yesterday's film. It was what he had been sure it would be; it was perfect. Laura was getting better and better, and Tom Leslie was superb. The others milked their bits to the ultimate, and the cameraman hadn't missed a nuance.

The cameraman had been Harry's choice, and Steve suddenly remembered Harry had come to prominence through the technical end of the business. Looking back on the pictures of Harry's he had seen, he remembered now how technically sound they had been.

But even the best cutter in the business could not have contrived the dramatic impact they had captured in yesterday's fought-for trip. Harry would be forced to admit that when he saw this film.

An empty day leered at him. He drove over to John Abbot's. He pulled up behind a green Pontiac and got out of his car as Tomkevic came down the walk from the house.

162

Steve stared at him. "Here, too? Are you crazy? Now what in hell are you doing here?"

Tomkevic's smile was cool. "It was your idea. You asked me to check the man and check his offer of money."

"Oh? And I'm under suspicion again? Or have I always been?"

"You're practically a partner of Bergdahl's, aren't you? You admitted seeing Jameson earlier that night. How do I know you went to a movie later? How do I know you weren't the man in the MG?"

"I don't have an MG."

"Your buddy, young Sidney, has. His car could be one place while he's establishing an alibi somewhere else, couldn't it?"

Steve said coldly, "You're really reaching now, aren't you? You're determined to twist this accident to suit your own purposes, no matter how absurd your theory actually is. Is that why Morton's free? Did you buy him a phony witness and then con the police into releasing him?"

"Watch your language, Leander. I can get rough, you know."

"Please do. Now and here." A redness moved through Steve's mind. "Fool me. Show me the guts I'm sure you lack. Get rough."

"Take it easy, Leander. Don't do anything foolish."

Steve took a step toward the investigator.

And from the lawn the gentle voice of John Abbot said, "That's right, Steve—don't do anything foolish."

Steve turned to stare at John. Abbot said to Tomkevic, "You'd better go. I think it would be wise if you went quietly and quickly."

"He doesn't scare me," Tomkevic said.

Abbot smiled. "Everyone is entitled to an occasional

163

error in judgment. Let me assure you that he's my best friend, but he scares me at the moment."

Tomkevic went away and the redness went with him and Steve stood on the walk trembling.

John came over to put a hand on his arm. "A drink will help. Lord, you looked—murderous. Aren't you ever going to learn to discipline that temper, Steve?"

"I have been disciplining it, John. Believe me, you'd be proud of me if you'd seen it. Ye gods, I've been getting along with Harry Bergdahl!"

Abbot chuckled. "You win. And I'll have to admit that Mr. Tomkevic even annoyed me for the few minutes he was here. What's happening that I don't know about?"

"Mix me a drink and I'll tell you," Steve answered. "Gosh, it's time for lunch, isn't it? I'd better phone Marcia."

"I'll phone her," Abbot said. "You sit down and relax. You're still trembling."

Steve had already mixed a drink when Abbot came back from phoning Marcia. Abbot went over to mix one for himself.

Steve asked, "Who's your wealthy friend who is willing to put money into a motion picture these days?"

"A man with money *and* faith," Abbot replied. "Johnson Waters."

"Money I knew he had," Steve said, "but not that much faith."

"He's always had faith in you, Steve. He's been in your fan club since your first picture."

Steve looked at his drink. "John, are we going to survive?"

"The industry, you mean? The present setup? Through exhibitors?"

"I mean without making pictures for TV."

"Of course we'll survive," Abbot said. "Forty years

ago a supposedly learned man assured me the movies meant the death of the publishing business. And a little later all the bright ones were positive that radio would ruin the record business. I hope you don't think a commercial-studded wrestling match will ever replace Laurence Olivier."

"That's hardly a fair comparison," Steve said.

"I'm not trying to be fair," Abbot told him smilingly. "It's my industry I'm defending."

"You know who else believes in it?"

"Harry Bergdahl. Is that who you meant?"

Steve nodded.

Abbot said, "There are angles to this business Harry knows very well. And he knows another very important thing—he knows enough not to interfere with a competent subordinate."

"That isn't his reputation. He has a reputation as a meddler."

"He's had to be. He rarely had competent subordinates. He never paid enough to get them. When cheap pictures sold, Harry made cheap pictures. He has never before had any reason to make a good one."

Steve smiled. "What a switch . . . You were the man who warned me against him."

"Because I knew you and I knew his reputation, and I felt that in a showdown, he'd win. I overlooked one of your less obvious attributes."

"What's that, John?"

"You're a con man. You're glib and occasionally tricky."

"Thanks," Steve said wryly.

"Well, aren't you?"

"Maybe. Yup, I guess. At times. When I have to be." He held up his empty glass.

"Mix your own," Abbot said mildly. "You don't scare me."

165

They had lunch together, and the reminiscences of John Abbot were not boring today. They were the background of a continuing industry, the colorful, impressive, illuminating history of a giant now sick but far from dead.

Steve left at two-thirty and drove toward home. But as he drove along Wilshire, an impulse moved him and he turned toward Brentwood. Mitchell Morton's Plymouth was parked in front of his apartment building. Steve sat in his own car for seconds before going up to turn the mechanical chime.

Morton came to the door in T-shirt and polished cotton Ivy League trousers. He stared at Steve without speaking.

"We'll shoot your bit tomorrow," Steve told him. "We want to get it into the can before you go to jail."

"I don't think I'm going to jail," Morton said calmly. "I had to tell some kind of story, didn't I?"

"Who's paying for Leon Spangler? Not you, working at minimum."

Morton didn't answer.

Steve said, "Patience, that's all you needed. The talent you have. You had to work a short cut. You're young. What was your hurry?"

"I don't understand you, Mr. Leander."

"You understand me. That lie about the MG, was that malice?"

Morton colored.

Steve asked, "How much did Tomkevic pay you to stooge for him?"

"That's enough, Mr. Leander. I don't need you."

"Don't you? I'll bet you'll show up for that part tomorrow, though. Show me some integrity; spit in my face."

Morton asked quietly, "Why? I don't have to prove

166

anything. I know you're as scared as I am. I've known that for a week."

The redness came to Steve again, and his hands clenched. The vision of Mitchell Morton wavered—and the door closed. He held onto the guard rail as he went down the steps.

At home Marcia was in the kitchen with Mrs. Burke. She told him, "Dave called. He wants you to phone him back."

"Is he home or at Bergdahl's?"

"I imagine he's home or he would have mentioned he wasn't. His phone number's in that little black book attached to the telephone book."

Dave, too, had an unlisted number. For a moment that casual thought stirred something in Steve's unconscious mind but brought forth nothing tangible. He dialed the number.

Dave said, "I have a visitor, a young actor. He's a friend of mine. He was on a double date with Pat Cullum last Wednesday night. He came to me for advice."

"Why? He knows his duty, doesn't he?"

A pause. "He doesn't want to make any enemies."

"Then he's in the wrong business. In this business, a man's reputation is established by making the right enemies. You're not *personally* afraid of what he might tell the police, are you, Dave?"

"Of course not. All right, I'll tell him to go directly to Sergeant Morrow. That's the man to see, isn't it?"

"Right. And tell him not to talk to Tomkevic at all."

"That's for sure." Dave lowered his voice. "Steve, when did you develop this new faith in Uncle Harry?"

Steve laughed. "When I learned we were brothers."

"Okay, Uncle Steve. I'll see you tomorrow."

"Early," Steve reminded him. "That scene of Morton's needs some polishing." He hung up before Dave could protest.

167

Outside, the sun was breaking through the overcast. In the kitchen Marcia asked, "More shenanigans?"

Steve glanced openly and meaningly at the kitchen extension.

"No, no," Marcia protested. "I could hear you from the living room. I heard you mention the police."

He told her about his conversation with Dave.

She sighed. "Harry Bergdahl and Steven Leander, that's a pair you can draw to, as Tom Duggan would say."

"It's a winning pair," Steve said. "With Dave, it makes a very potent three-of-a-kind."

"That I'll buy," she agreed. "Three egocentric monsters."

Mrs. Burke said, "You shouldn't talk like that, Mrs. Leander. I don't know this Mr. Bergdahl, but Mr. Sidney and your husband are as fine a pair of men as it has ever been my privilege to meet."

Steve smiled smugly. "Mrs. Burke, you have just earned yourself a free trip to the early show at the Bay. Mrs. Leander and I are going out for dinner this evening."

Marcia said sadly, "And then to a movie, I suppose? Couldn't we think of some better entertainment for a change?"

"There is no better entertainment," Steve said, "anywhere in the world."

And Mrs. Burke nodded in complete agreement.

EIGHTEEN

Mitchell Morton was an actor. Despite the turmoil of his recent publicity and aware that the man directing him hated him, it would have been logical to expect some garbled lines and wooden gestures from him Friday morning. Nothing of the sort happened. He moved through the scene with a touch reminiscent of Tom Leslie and, like Tom, he brought the others in the scene up to his dramatic level. He finished faultlessly in one take.

Dave said quietly to Steve, "Hard man to hate, isn't he?"

Steve nodded. "A damned fool, a talented damned fool."

"Maybe he's not so foolish," Dave pointed out. "Somebody with money is certainly paying for his lawyer."

Morton came over to ask, "All right, Mr. Leander?"

"Excellent, Mr. Morton." Steve nodded a dismissal and turned away.

Morton stood there stubbornly. "You don't give a man any breaks, do you?"

Steve looked at him coldly. "Don't I? You worked this morning, didn't you? I overlooked your first disreputable approach to me, didn't I? Exactly how many breaks do you think you're entitled to, Morton?"

They stood there silently a moment, staring at each other. Then Dave said, "Let's go to lunch, Steve. It's time for lunch."

169

Something stirred in Steve's unconscious mind again, and this time it came to the surface. He watched Morton walk away and he said to Dave, "Something just occurred to me."

"What?"

"When Morton phoned me, he said he got my telephone number from Hart Jameson. He couldn't have. Jameson didn't have it."

Dave said, "There are people who make a business of selling unlisted phone numbers. He probably bought it."

Steve nodded absently and began to enumerate in his mind those people who had his phone number. Dave, Harry, Laura. If Morton had bought his number, there would be no reason for him not to admit it. A man attempting blackmail wouldn't be reluctant to admit he bought an unlisted telephone number.

Harry joined them in the commissary for lunch. "How did the bastard do?" he asked.

Steve smiled. "I've got bad news for you, Harry. He was great."

Harry sighed. He looked at the tablecloth. "I—that film you shot Wednesday, Steve, it was—well . . ." He shook his head.

Dave supplied "Spectacular? Sensational? Superb? A producer shouldn't run out of superlatives, Uncle Harry."

Harry frowned. "So I've been wrong before. You know somebody who hasn't? You young snots . . ."

Steve asked, "Did you ever give Hart Jameson my telephone number, Harry?"

Bergdahl stared. "I don't remember. No, I'm sure I didn't. Are we on that kick again? The picture, the picture, the picture—let's think about the *picture*. Okay?"

Steve winked. "Okay, boss."

170

Across the table from them, Dave said, "And I didn't give it to him. So that leaves who, Steve?"

"Only Laura," Steve answered.

"The picture," Harry said ominously.

"The picture *and* Laura," Steve said. "She's doing well, isn't she, Harry?"

Bergdahl nodded. "And we know why, don't we? You almost got her an Academy Award the first time you directed her."

"How sweet of you to remember," Steve said. "I'll remind you of it next time we tangle." He buttered a roll carefully. "Harry, I've been thinking of that money John Abbot was talking about."

Harry looked up suspiciously. "So . . . ?"

"Johnson Water's the man with the money," Steve went on. "I was thinking if we didn't need it for this picture, it would be a shame to let it go to waste, wouldn't it?"

Harry looked less suspicious. "So . . . ?"

"We ought to get it for our next picture."

Surprise wiped out the remnants of suspicion on Harry's face. "*We . . . ? Our* next picture? Why am I in?"

"Because I'm not a producer, yet. I've a few hard facts to learn about economy and audience acceptance before I take that jump. You're a good producer."

Bergdahl said nothing. A variety of emotions seemed to play over his broad face.

Dave said lightly, "I know an available screenwriter."

Bergdahl smiled. "A *cheap* available screenwriter?"

The afternoon moved less smoothly than the morning had, but it was far from wasted. It had been another good day.

Steve drove home with an unreasonable sense of premonition. Things were going too well; he had an adolescent uneasiness about smooth sailing.

It was a hot day and Marcia was in the pool. He put on his trunks and went down to join her. He dived deeply and stayed under, swimming toward her legs.

They had a few drinks on the sundeck after their swim and it was eight o'clock before they sat down to dinner. At eight-twenty Dave phoned.

He said, "You'd better get that lawyer you were bragging about. Sergeant Morrow has just come out here and picked up Uncle Harry."

"Why? What happened now?"

"They located that perfume man. Uncle Harry is the real customer for that Number 263."

"What does that prove? They must have something else."

"Probably. Morrow looked confident. Could you run over here after you phone the lawyer? Dotty's—unnerved. I'm going down to Headquarters."

In the background Dotty said, "Stop that, Dave. I don't need anyone to hold my hand."

The words triggered an incident in Steve's memory. He said, "I'll get right over there. I'll be there in twenty minutes."

"I'll leave now then," Dave said.

Steve hung up and stood by the phone, thinking back.

From the dining room Marcia called, "What's the matter, Steve? What's happened?"

He came back to the dining room. "I've been stupid. I overlooked the obvious. The police have just picked up Harry Bergdahl."

"That isn't what you meant by overlooking the obvious. What did you mean by that?"

"I meant I've been as blind as Tomkevic. I want you to phone my lawyer, Craig Medoff, and tell him Harry's been picked up. I'm going over to Bergdahl's."

She stood up. "All right. But what did you overlook?"

"The girl in Hart's apartment. You stay here; Harry

may phone. And call Medoff right now." He went out to the car.

Dotty opened the door to Steve's ring. She seemed to be swaying and her voice was thick. "I appreciate your coming."

He grinned at her. "That isn't what you told Dave."

"I didn't think it was necessary," she enunciated very carefully. "There was no point in disrupting your evening. Harry's not in serious trouble anyway, is he?"

Steve followed her into the living room. "Of course not. Morrow was probably egged on by Tomkevic to make a grandstand play. There'll be some red faces in the morning, I guarantee you."

Dotty nodded. "I thought so. Would you like a drink?"

"I could use one. Bourbon and water."

She mixed a pair. She was ludicrously careful as she poured the whiskey, added water, and slowly walked to the davenport with both of them. She handed him one and sat a few feet from him.

Steve chuckled. "I can see Harry now, giving them all hell. There'll be a false arrest suit filed, I'll bet."

Dotty said nothing. Her smile was labored.

Steve said, "I had a weird idea this afternoon. Are you superstitious?"

She shook her head. She sipped her drink and stared at him.

Steve said, "Pat Cullum had a small part in this picture we're making. Why don't you take it?"

"I'm not an actress," she said heavily. "I gave up my career."

"Because you don't need the money now, married to Harry. But just for fun? As a gag?"

She shook her head stubbornly.

"It's only a line," Steve explained. "You're supposed

173

to be a little tipsy, see? And this fellow is talking on the phone, but he's well—fondling you at the same time. And you giggle and say 'Stop that!' You'd have fun doing it and . . ."

"Shut up," Dotty said. She glared at him.

Steve shrugged and sipped his drink. Dotty finished hers and went over to pour another.

Steve said, "Somebody told me that Harry met Jameson through you. Is that right?"

She nodded and sat down on the davenport again with a full glass.

"You knew Morton, too? Through Jameson?"

She said nothing.

Steve sipped his drink. "Tomkevic was sure Harry knew Morton, but it was you who knew him. Did you give him my phone number?"

"I don't know what you're talking about," she said warily.

"Morton told me yesterday that he didn't need me. Was that because he thought he could get to Harry through you? Are you paying for his attorney?"

She stared at the fireplace.

He asked gently, "Don't you want to talk, Dotty?"

She shook her head.

"Do you mind if I do?"

"Suit yourself."

Steve leaned back. "What Morrow overlooked is that when a man buys perfume, he buys the kind *he* likes, quite often. He likes to smell it on his women, on all of his women. Do you wear Dostel Number 263, Dotty?"

She shook her head.

"Harry bought you some. Didn't you ever wear it?"

She stared at the fireplace.

"What I overlooked," Steve went on, "was the obvious fact that Jameson was no gentleman. There would

174

be no point in his hiding a woman just because I came to visit him. Not unless I knew the woman, and she wanted to hide."

Dotty turned her head. "What are you trying to prove, Steve? What can you prove?"

"I'm just expounding a theory. Does it bore you?"

She shook her head slowly.

"And another thing," he continued, "Jameson didn't worry about the girl overhearing the accident gimmick. That could indicate the girl already knew it. Through her husband?"

Dotty turned to face him again.

"What beats me," Steve said thoughtfully, "is why the girl would want to kill him."

Dotty said carefully, "Maybe she didn't. Maybe they were both crazy drunk and Jameson bragged about how easy it would be to ride on the edge of the bluff and the girl got scared and jumped out of the car and ran away."

"And was picked up by Mitchell Morton," Steve went on, "and taken home. And Mitchell tried to blackmail her. He didn't want much, just a part in the picture. And the girl said it would look suspicious coming through her. She suggested he phone Steven Leander and tell him that he knew something the police should. And the girl gave Morton my number."

"And what difference does it make?" Dotty asked hoarsely. "It's still an accident, isn't it?"

"Yes," Steve agreed, "it certainly is. Can I mix you another drink?"

"I've had too many already," she said. "Why don't you leave?"

"All right." He finished his drink and stood up. "What you forget is that Morton is an actor and an ambitious one. His allegiance is going to go to the person who can do him the most good. Unfortunately, you're not a producer."

175

She stared at him. "No, but with Pat Cullum dead, Harry has only his little Dotty, hasn't he? With Pat Cullum dead, Dotty is again queen; and if I tell Harry I want Mitchell Morton out of the business, what do you think will happen?"

Steve said softly, "Is that why you killed her? Don't you think there will be other Pat Cullums? Don't you think this town is loaded with them?"

"There'll never be another Pat Cullum," Dotty said. "I can guarantee you that. Harry and I have talked it over very carefully, and there will never be another Pat Cullum. She was the first infidelity in our marriage and now she's dead. I don't know who killed her, but I'm glad she's dead. Harry's mine now, *all mine.*"

"You know who killed her, Dotty. You did. And it was senseless. Because you can't control Harry forever. He's just not that kind of man. He has to dominate."

Dotty smiled blearily and shook her head.

Steve asked, "Was Morton working for you when he took out Pat Cullum? Did you send him over to find out how she'd learned the mystery girl was wearing your perfume?"

"I know how she found that out," Dotty said thickly. "You told her. She was going to tell the police about that, too, about the perfume. She threatened me with that."

"And then you killed her?"

"I didn't kill her. I didn't, I didn't, I didn't . . ." Her voice rose hysterically and her head shook savagely. "You can't prove I killed her. *Nobody* can prove that!"

"I can prove you had reason to. Do you want to tell me about it?"

Dotty's impressive bosom rose and fell. "Hart Jameson's death was an accident. That's God's gospel truth. When you told Pat Cullum about the perfume, she knew I must have been the girl with Hart that night, the mysterious missing woman."

"Did she threaten you with that?"

Dotty took a deep breath and looked at Steve anxiously. "She did. She said if it ever came out, it would ruin me. It could send me to prison. She told me that if I interfered with her—her *romance* she called it—her affair with *my* husband, she would tell the police I was with Hart Jameson the night he died."

Steve stared. "She—threatened you? My God, did she think Harry was going to marry her?"

Dotty nodded mutely, her eyes beseechingly on Steve. "The silly little tramp thought Harry would divorce me. Steve, I swear to you Hart Jameson's death was an accident. He was showing off. He was always showing off."

Steve looked at the carpeting and up at Dotty. "You haven't told the whole truth, Dotty. You've admitted Pat threatened you. Well, Morton has already told me that you killed her."

"You're a liar," she said hoarsely. "You're trying to trick me. I can have you destroyed, too, Steve. I know about you and Pat Cullum. I can ruin your marriage."

Steve shook his head. "Why don't you come with me to the police? Harry must suspect, too. You claimed to be worried about him, but in reality he was worried about you. He knows, doesn't he?"

"I don't have to listen to any more of this," she whispered. "Get out of my house."

"I'm going. I'm sure the police will listen more politely than you did. Good night, Dotty."

He was halfway to the door when she whimpered, "Steve, wait—Steve, please . . ."

By the time he got back to the davenport, she had passed out. He went to the phone and called Headquarters. He asked for Sergeant Morrow.

"Sergeant Morrow is busy at the moment, sir. May I be of help?"

"No," Steve answered. "This concerns the murder of the Cullum girl, and I will talk only to Sergeant Morrow. Tell him Steven Leander is on the phone."

"One moment, sir."

It was a little longer than that before Morrow came on. Steve said, "I want you to try something. I want you to pull in Mitchell Morton and tell him Mrs. Bergdahl has confessed to everything. Tell him there's no point in his sticking to that ridiculous story of his."

"We don't have to pull him in; he's down here. What kind of a game are you trying to run now, Leander?"

"Sergeant, have you considered that all those fingers that pointed at Harry Bergdahl were really only pointing at his house? Get Morton alone and tell him what I've told you to, and I guarantee you'll come up with something solid."

"Where's Mrs. Bergdahl now?"

"Ten feet from me. Dead drunk and fast asleep. As soon as one of your men gets here to her house, I'll come down. Don't let Bergdahl know what you're questioning Morton about."

A silence.

Steve said, "How much help do you need, Sergeant? Haven't I given you enough even before tonight?"

"All right. *All right!*"

From the direction of the davenport Dotty Bergdahl moaned in her sleep.

The room was as dreary as the little room in the Hollywood station, but this one was bigger. Harry and Steve sat on chairs against the wall. Dave sat behind the desk.

Detective Sommers came in to tell them, "I guess you

can all go home. That Morton is singing like a para-keet."

Harry said gruffly, "Who can believe him? You flat-feet ain't had enough experience with that bastard? That don't mean my wife had anything to do with Miss Cullum's death."

Sommers looked at him compassionately. "We don't need Morton for that, Mr. Bergdahl. We had some prints from the girl's apartment we've been trying to match up." His voice was lower. "Your wife fills the bill."

Harry took a deep breath and stared at the floor. Sommers went out.

Dave said, "We'd better get home, Uncle Harry. It's late."

Harry nodded, still staring at the floor. "The little bitch. The dirty little bitch."

Steve came over to put a hand on his shoulder. "You can always get another wife, Harry. We've got more important things to worry about. We've got a picture to finish."

ABOUT THE AUTHOR

WILLIAM CAMPBELL GAULT says that he has only one major regret in his life, namely, that he wasn't born rich in California and an early investor in real estate there. Otherwise his first forty years in Milwaukee were pleasant and the last eight in California even more so. After attending the University of Wisconsin, he engaged in various business enterprises and finally moved to California, where he settled in Pacific Palisades not far from a good country club where he could play golf as often as deadlines on his books would allow. He says that he is a bad golfer and a fair Republican, and leads a very quiet life except for those "mild poker games with other gaming citizens" in his neighborhood. He served in the 166th Infantry and spent most of his military career in Hawaii.

Mr. Gault has a nine-year-old daughter who is studying the cello and a nineteen-year-old son who is on a four-year General Motors Scholarship at Holy Cross. Recently the family moved to Santa Barbara. He adds that his wife does all the cooking but "helps him with the dishes almost every evening."

This is his tenth book, including the Brock (the Rock) Callahan series. His later stories, all placed in the Los Angeles area, shed some new rays of light on the folkways of that region.

Printed in the United States
By Bookmasters